Can't resist a sexy military hero?
*Then you'll love our **Uniformly Hot!** miniseries.*

*Harlequin Blaze's bestselling miniseries
continues with more irresistible heroes
from all branches of the armed forces.*

Don't miss

BRING ME TO LIFE
by Kira Sinclair
December 2014

SEDUCING THE MARINE
by Kate Hoffmann
January 2015

A SEAL'S SECRET
by Tawny Weber
February 2015

Dear Reader,

I'm so excited to be visiting Sweetheart, South Carolina, again! What's not to love about a small Southern town with quaint charm, great friends... and *very* hot men? From the moment Tatum Huntley popped onto the pages in *The Risk-Taker* I knew she was hiding a story behind that sarcastic wit. And like any good writer, I wanted to figure out what made her that way. I wasn't quite prepared when Evan, a badass on a Harley, showed up after three long years of her thinking him dead. He nearly sent strong, independent Tatum to her knees with hope and fear and longing.

No one escapes life without being touched by grief. We've all lost someone we cared deeply for...a grandparent, parent, lover, friend. Heartache is a universal emotion. However, it can help us appreciate the people and time we have on this earth. I don't know anyone who would balk at having a few more hours—or even minutes—with someone they've lost. But the reality isn't quite so idyllic when Evan roars back into Tatum's life. Losing him devastated Tatum. And letting him in once more means risking that pain all over again. But how can she resist falling for the man she's always loved?

Bring Me to Life is all about the power of second chances and seizing those miracles that we're all blessed with on occasion. I hope you enjoy Tatum and Evan's story! I'd love to hear from you at kirasinclair.com, or come chat with me on Twitter.

Best wishes,

Kira

Bring Me to Life

—

Kira Sinclair

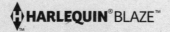

Recycling programs
for this product may
not exist in your area.

ISBN-13: 978-0-373-79828-5

Bring Me to Life

Printed in U.S.A.

H HARLEQUIN®
TM www.Harlequin.com

Kira Sinclair is an award-winning author who writes emotional, passionate contemporary romances. Double winner of the National Readers' Choice Award, her first foray into writing fiction was for a high-school English assignment. Nothing could dampen her enthusiasm...not even being forced to read the love story aloud to the class. However, it definitely made her blush. Writing about striking, sexy heroes and passionate, determined women has always excited her. She lives with her two beautiful daughters in North Alabama. Kira loves to hear from readers at kirasinclair.com.

Books by Kira Sinclair

Harlequin Blaze

Whispers in the Dark
Afterburn
Caught Off Guard
What Might Have Been
Bring It On
Take It Down
Rub It In
The Risk-Taker
She's No Angel
The Devil She Knows
Captivate Me
Testing the Limits

To get the inside scoop on Harlequin Blaze and its talented writers, be sure to check out blazeauthors.com.

All backlist available in ebook format.

I'd like to dedicate this book to my parents.

My life took an unexpected turn in the middle of writing this book, and I wouldn't have been able to get through each day without their unconditional love and support. I've always known I was blessed with the best parents in the world. Growing up, I didn't always make life easy, but they never wavered in their support of me and my decisions... even when they didn't agree with them. They've shown me, by example, what a good parent should be, how a good person should live and what a strong relationship should look like.

Love you both!

1

THROUGH THE RAINBOW slivers of colored glass, Tatum Huntley watched soft, fluffy snowflakes drift down from the darkened sky to blanket the dead grass surrounding the church. The scene was beautiful, just like everything else about Hope's wedding day had been.

She wanted that for her friend, the perfect day to celebrate the love she'd found and fought for with her husband, Gage.

Behind Tatum, the background noise of her friends' chattering voices was both soothing and a little abrasive. They were helping Hope gather the last of her things so she and Gage could head out on their honeymoon.

Any other time, Tatum would have been right in the middle of the laughter and friendly ribbing, making an inappropriate comment or slipping a sex toy into Hope's luggage as a joke—anything to have her friend blushing.

But tonight Tatum couldn't muster the energy to pretend everything was okay.

There was no way for her friends to know how

much this day ripped at raw emotions. Hell, she hadn't realized it would affect her this much.

It wasn't as if she and Evan had had a perfect, white, church wedding. They'd gone to the courthouse with a handful of their friends gathered around as witnesses. Sure, she'd worn a white dress, but it had been off the rack and nothing like the confection Willow had designed for Hope. And her bouquet had been a simple mix of spring flowers they'd picked up at a local florist on the way.

Far from Hope and Gage's extravaganza. Although, she probably should have assumed…she'd loved Evan with every single cell in her body, just as Hope loved Gage. Their days definitely shared that.

But Hope, Lexi, Willow, Macey, none of them even knew she'd been married. And that was the way she wanted it.

No one in her current life knew her past—it was the whole reason she'd bought Petals, become a florist and moved to Sweetheart, South Carolina. Here she could pretend her life was okay, that her heart hadn't been ripped from her body and stomped on by fate and some military mission she didn't have the clearance to know the details about.

Her floral business gave her a purpose, a reason to get up every morning and keep going.

Tatum's focus shifted to the reflection of her friends in the window, and she tried to pull her emotions back from the brink of melancholy. Hope didn't deserve her moping.

Taking a deep breath, she pushed the sad memories deep beneath a layer of false bravado. Later. She could wallow later.

Willow was fussing with Hope's train, repositioning the long layers of silk she'd pulled up into a bustle. Even now, after the ceremony and a large chunk of the reception were already over, she couldn't seem to keep her hands off the dress.

Reaching behind her, Hope grasped Willow's arm and pulled her back onto her feet. With exasperation, she said, "Will you please leave it alone? You aren't supposed to be working. You're my bridesmaid not my dress designer."

A frown tugged Willow's dark brows. "Can't I be both?"

"Not if it means you're on your hands and knees while the rest of us are sipping champagne."

Willow sighed, looked longingly at the folded edges of the train—that from Tatum's point of view looked perfect—and then studiously turned her back on it, taking one of the glasses of sparkling wine.

"Hope, are you ready to go?" Gage's deep voice came from the other side of the closed door.

"Just a minute," she called, twirling with a swish of material against the floor.

She grabbed the last two glasses of wine, and thrust a cool flute into Tatum's empty hand.

Flinging an arm around her shoulders, Hope beckoned everyone close. They crowded together, a tight circle of people Tatum hadn't known existed a few years ago.

Now they were her best friends. Her strength.

Hope's gaze traveled around the circle, her eyes going misty. "I love you guys. Thank you for being part of my day and making sure it was perfect."

There were murmurs and answering tears, glasses clinking and gulps of champagne.

And then Hope was gone, folded beneath Gage's arm and ushered out into the chilly December night.

Tatum trailed slowly behind the other girls as they rushed to watch the newly married couple race for the waiting car ready to drive them into Charleston to catch their flight.

Hope and Gage rushed through a gauntlet of bubbles mixed with snowflakes and ringing good wishes. Tatum stood at the top of the steps, watching the scene below, unable to fight the sensation that she was on the outside looking in.

When she'd first moved to town, that sensation had been pretty much constant. As a transplanted Yankee—from Detroit, no less—arriving in Sweetheart had felt a little like landing on another planet. But that's what she'd needed. A fresh start. Something completely new.

In the last two years, the out-of-place sensation had faded to little more than an unpleasant memory. Until tonight. Something about tonight had made her feel off-kilter.

Grasping the edges of the black velvet shrug that accompanied her deep burgundy dress, Tatum hugged herself. She thought she was alone, everyone else focused on Hope and Gage's escape, until a soft hand landed on her hip.

Startled, she gave a little jerk as Willow's arm settled around her waist.

"Hey, chickie, you've been quiet tonight. Wanna tell me what's up?"

For the briefest moment, Tatum thought about unloading on her friend, telling her every second of anguish and anger she'd dealt with over the last three years. But that wouldn't exactly be fair.

She shook her head. "It's nothing."

Willow squeezed, pulling her in tighter. "You know I'm not buying that lie, right?"

"It isn't a lie."

"Oh, it is. But I'll let you get away with it. For now."

Below them, Hope folded into the backseat of the car, yanking the voluminous layers of skirt in after her. Willow cringed, making a small, wounded whimper.

Tatum's mouth twitched. Finding something to smile about was a gift she hadn't expected, even if it had come at Willow's sense of affront as the dress's designer.

It was her turn to wrap a comforting arm around Willow's shoulders. "Maybe it would be better if you didn't watch."

With a resigned sigh, Willow said, "No, I want to see them leave."

The driver closed the car door and ran around to the front. Trails of steam hit the cold air and billowed from the tailpipe, leaving a hazy cloud behind as he finally pulled away.

The minute the car disappeared, people streamed past Tatum into the reception, rushing for warmth, another slice of cake and a chance to enjoy the DJ waiting to crank the party up another notch and let them dance into the wee hours of the morning.

But Tatum couldn't move to follow them.

Her body was frozen, her eyes trained on the vision of a ghost, propped against the sleek chrome of a badass bike parked against the curb across the street.

He couldn't be real. It must be her imagination. Memories. And possibly too much champagne.

Although, that didn't stop the frantic pace of her heart as it picked up inside her chest. Her body turned hot and then cold. She couldn't breathe. Tears pricked the back of her eyelids, just as painful as the day she'd learned he was gone.

Why would her imagination play such a cruel joke?

She'd forgotten Willow was beside her, until her arm tightened around Tatum's waist. "Who is that guy?" her friend asked.

Tatum's mouth and tongue wouldn't work.

Willow grasped her hand. "Are you okay? You've gone seriously pale."

Somehow, she found the power to whisper, "You can see him?"

"You mean the guy with the bike staring at you like he wants to throw you on the back and race away? Yeah, I can see him. Why wouldn't I be able to?"

"Because that's my husband...and he's dead."

SHE LOOKED AS though she'd seen a ghost, which was pretty much true.

No, she looked amazing, but then Tatum always had. Different, but that was to be expected. It had been three years.

They'd both changed.

Evan watched her, waiting. Beneath the lie of his relaxed posture, his body was strung tight.

There was no way to anticipate her reaction. Although he'd sure as hell tried.

In the dark moments, the ones where he thought it might have been better if he had died on that night three years ago, she had been the only thing that had drawn him back from the brink. When he'd watched men, women and children killed in front of him. Hell, when he'd done the killing, trying to justify his actions by remembering the men dying deserved what they had gotten.

The memory of her had kept him going—her rasping laughter, the rare times when her eyes danced with delight and the feel of her body rubbing against his, reminding him there were good things in the world. And that once, before his life had turned to shit, he'd been a part of them.

Evan desperately needed her now. Needed the connection to what he'd left behind.

Without it, he was afraid the darkness would swallow him for good.

Tatum stared at him, a jumble of emotions melting one into another—shock, relief, anger, resolve.

A woman, wearing the same long burgundy dress and velvet wrap as his wife, stood beside her. Tatum murmured something he couldn't hear. The other woman rocked back on her heels as if she'd been hit, her eyes going wide. She sputtered, wrapped her arm around Tatum's waist and pulled her tight into the protective shield of her body.

He had no idea who the woman was, but it was obvious she cared about his wife. He was glad. He'd worried about Tatum so much. Hated that his choices had hurt her. Left her alone. But there was no way he could have prevented it.

In true Tatum fashion, she allowed the comforting embrace only for a moment before pulling out of the hold.

That was his wife. She hid her soft, gooey center beneath a steely hard shell. Life had taught her how to protect herself.

It hurt knowing his "death" had only reinforced the lessons.

Tatum's feet shuffled. Was she going to head back into the group of buildings behind her and pretend he didn't exist or walk across the street and deal with him? He wasn't entirely certain.

Apparently, neither was she. Her body hesitated, moving forward and then pulling back several times before she actually took a step toward him. One led to two and three and then a rush of a handful more. She raced across the pavement, her heels clicking against the ice-slicked asphalt.

Evan straightened, spreading his feet wide and dropping his arms to his sides.

Her long dress spun out around her legs, fluttering in the breeze caused by her flight. He braced, thinking she was going to launch herself at him. His heart stuttered, hope and happiness—the first he'd allowed himself to indulge in for a very long time—bubbled up through his chest.

But she didn't throw herself into his waiting arms.

Instead, she reached back, put every ounce of power behind her shoulder and slapped the shit out of him.

The ringing crack of palm against cheek broke through the night. His head snapped sideways. Evan groaned, an involuntary sound that tore through his throat.

"Bastard," she hissed.

Cradling his jaw with a hand, Evan slowly righted his body.

Tatum shook out her fingers as she glared at him through tempting, flashing green eyes. Eyes that had haunted both his nightmares and dreams. The worst had been the nightmares where he was certain the enemy had found her, torturing her as revenge for the lies he'd told.

Evan barely registered the other woman hovering behind them. He knew she was there, but he couldn't drag his gaze away from Tatum long enough to notice her. He'd hoped not to have an audience for this reunion.

"I buried you," Tatum said. "I stood beside your sobbing mother and father and buried you. For months, I visited your grave, bringing flowers and talking to you, sharing how hard it was to move on and let you go."

"I know," he whispered. The anguish in her voice and eyes killed him. What he wanted to do was hold her close, offer her the comfort of his body. Something told him that wouldn't go over well.

Her eyes flashed. "Where the hell have you been for the last three years?"

"Colombia."

"And I don't suppose they had cell phones, or email or, hell, a post office in Colombia?"

He thought the anguish was bad, but the caustic rage was ten times worse. It made his chest ache with helplessness. He didn't like to feel helpless.

"Let me explain."

"Oh, you're definitely going to do that. But not now. Not here. This is my friend's wedding and I will not ruin the rest of their party with your drama. You've waited this long, one more night won't hurt."

Evan wasn't entirely certain of that. The moment the Army had released him, he'd hightailed it to Sweetheart, not even bothering to stop for a change of clothes.

He'd been in the States for a little over a week, relating the specifics of his deep-cover mission to some arrogant prick who'd never seen a dirty, dangerous

day of battle in his life. Not to mention helping tie up
the loose ends after single-handedly dismantling one
of the most bloodthirsty and ruthless drug cartels in
Colombia. And going ape-shit crazy because the bu-
reaucrats in charge were taking their sweet time and
wouldn't flippin' release him.

His wife had been so close, and he hadn't been able
to get to her. Beyond frustrating.

The other bridesmaid stepped up beside Tatum, her
voice soft and soothing as she said, "I'm sure everyone would understand if you needed to leave, Tatum.
Hope and Gage are already gone."

"Maybe, but that's beside the point, Willow." His
wife's hands fisted at her sides.

Evan shifted away, putting a little more space between them just in case she decided she needed to use
them on him.

It struck him as hilarious that he'd spent the last
three years rubbing elbows with some of the most
hardened criminals in South America, constantly wondering if today was the day he'd end up with a bullet
in the back, and taken the inherent danger in stride.

But a pissed off Tatum? She scared the shit out of
him. Always had. She didn't hesitate to fight dirty.
It was one of the things he'd always loved about her.
And hated, since life had taught her the need and skills
to do it.

Her gaze darted from him to Willow and back
again. Her mouth thinned and her eyes snapped. Finally, she growled, "Dammit!" She poked a finger into
his chest. "Stay here." She wrapped a hand around
Willow's arm and dragged the other woman behind
her.

Willow didn't turn, not right away, but let her gaze

trail down his entire body as she walked backward. In heels several inches high. Over ice-covered pavement. He might have been impressed, if he hadn't been so conscious of the fact she was weighing and measuring him while she was doing it.

And her dark, calm eyes gave no indication just how he'd scored.

Evan watched Tatum and Willow disappear inside, heavy doors slamming shut behind them.

It was entirely possible she was screwing with him and had every intention of letting him freeze his ass off waiting on her while she whooped it up at the party.

But he didn't think so. Tatum was the kind of woman who faced problems head on, always had been. She didn't hide her head in the sand or pretend something wasn't happening in the hope the problem would disappear. She made a decision and took action.

It was a trait they shared, something he'd always admired about her.

Crossing his arms over his chest, Evan leaned back against the seat of his bike. His gaze wandered up and down the street. It was quiet, just like the rest of the small southern town.

He had to admit, Sweetheart, South Carolina, was the last place he'd expected to find Tatum. She was a big-city girl. Growing up in Detroit, her family had lived paycheck to paycheck, close enough to the edge of disaster to make life a little unpredictable.

Her senior year of high school, her dad had lost his manufacturing job, sending her family into turmoil. Her dreams of college were crushed, at least for a little while.

Evan had watched her struggle that last year to

hold everyone together. She'd been the glue keeping her mother and father moving forward.

He'd joined the Army right out of high school. They'd married a few weeks later, mostly to give Tatum his benefits, although he'd known for years he had wanted to marry her. The timeline had just been bumped up by circumstances.

He'd gone off to basic training and she'd stayed behind, working and trying to keep things going back home with her parents. Her mother being diagnosed with ovarian cancer was just one more blow. Without insurance, they couldn't afford treatment. She did get some, but it wasn't enough, and she died a year later. Her father, snowed under beneath the weight of grief and debt, had committed suicide.

Tatum was the one who'd found him, walking into a bloody mess.

Evan would never forget that phone call. By then, he'd been stationed in Iraq, living apart from the wife he loved, unable to comfort or help her the way he had wanted.

She hadn't been hysterical, not his Tatum. Although, no matter how strong she'd tried to be, she had been unable to hide the pain locked deep inside. Or the relief, guilt and anger. Not from him.

She'd been carrying such a heavy burden at so young an age. And Evan had wanted more than anything to be there for her, to hold her and shoulder some of that weight.

He'd taken leave, come home and helped her deal with the financial mess her father had left behind. And he'd immediately moved her to North Carolina where he was stationed at Fort Bragg.

They had been happy. Sometimes she'd fought the

guilt of that, but he could always shake her out of the melancholy.

She had been the perfect military wife, independent, strong, with plans and goals of her own. Unlike some of the wives, she hadn't struggled when he was gone for long stretches of time. She had missed him, a lot, but they had plenty of experience dealing with separation. She had taken it all in stride, relishing the time they were able to spend together.

She had started college, eventually earning a business degree and going to work for a tech company. Special Ops had recruited him. Things had stabilized. They had been happy, had even started talking about kids.

Then, in the middle of an undercover drug op, their informant screwed his team and any hope of a future had crumbled. Their cover had been blown. Well, everyone's but his. The resulting shitstorm had descended so quickly there had been no way to prepare.

One minute they had all been fine and the next, several of his buddies lay in pools of blood, with him the only one left standing. He'd thought he was dead, too.

He shivered. This little trip down memory lane wasn't helping his mental state. He needed to be clear-headed for the conversation that was coming.

Purposely turning his focus back to his surroundings, he surveyed the town Tatum had chosen to call home. He could see the appeal of Sweetheart, even if it wasn't what either of them had grown up with. The place was like the background for a Norman Rockwell painting—everywhere he looked there were Christmas lights, fragrant garlands of evergreen and shiny red, green and gold hanging balls. With the light layer of snow blanketing everything and the huge flakes drifting slowly from the sky, the town looked perfectly ideal.

What had surprised him almost as much as the fact that Tatum had chosen Sweetheart was the reason she'd moved here—to buy the only florist shop in town, Petals.

Try as he might, he couldn't picture Tatum patiently arranging brightly colored flowers. She'd never been the overly romantic type.

But according to the info the Army had given him, she'd been doing it for about two years, using his insurance money to make the purchase.

One of the first things he'd done when he'd finally made contact was ensure no one would be able to come after her for that money. The company had paid out and the Army, who'd eventually known he was alive even if it had been several months later, had let them.

He'd been assured Tatum was protected. Surprisingly, he wasn't the first soldier to rise from the dead.

The front door squealed, old wood against old wood, and Tatum slipped through the opening. The dress was gone, replaced by a dark pair of jeans, boots with tufts of fuzz shooting from the top and a heavy coat that enveloped her body, hiding everything else from him beneath a wall of shiny, quilted blue.

A plastic bag that most likely held her dress was draped over her arm. Another bag was slung over her shoulder, smacking against her thigh with every second step.

Her steps were deliberate and silent. She stopped several feet away from him. Evan felt the space between them like the gulf of a river, the swirl of their history, her anger and his hope threatening to pull them under if either of them tried to bridge the gap.

Snowflakes clung to her dark lashes, sparkling in the scattered light from the lamppost close by. She stared at him for several seconds before shaking her head. "Where are you staying?"

"I don't know. I didn't stop long enough to figure that out, Tatum. The first chance I could, I hopped my bike and rode here."

She sucked in a deep breath. "The resort isn't open yet. You could stay at the B and B, but it's full of guests for Hope and Gage's wedding. I suppose you could drive back to Charleston."

"What about staying at your place?"

He watched Tatum's tongue sneak out and sweep across her parted lips. The vein just beneath her jaw pulsed with tension.

"Dammit," she muttered, so quiet he almost missed it.

"Tatum, we need to talk. I'll sleep on the couch if that's what you want."

Her mouth thinned. And then trembled. "If that's what I want? What am I supposed to want, Evan? You've been gone for three years."

Swallowing the huge knot lodged in his throat, he opened his mouth to ask the question he'd been dreading since the moment he knew he was going to make it out of Colombia alive.

It was the one thing he'd tried not to think about at all while he was down there—because any time he lost the battle, it would make him want to throw up. Even now, his stomach churned.

He knew she hadn't remarried. According to the intel he'd browbeaten a friend into getting him while he spun his wheels in Charleston, he knew no one lived with her. But that didn't mean she hadn't moved on.

"Is there someone in your life?"

"What?"

"Are you dating anyone?"

Her head snapped back. Her deep, emerald eyes widened. And then they narrowed.

"I'm not sure you have any right to ask me that, Evan."

The slimy reptiles slithering through his belly began to quiet. He took a single step toward her, and when she didn't counter with one backward, he took another and another until he stood right in front of her. Toe to toe, he stared into her upturned face.

Her creamy skin was warm when he reached for her, running the pad of a single finger over the slope of her cheekbone.

"What I want is to kiss my wife. What I want is to pull her into my arms and taste her mouth. Feel the silky, smooth texture of her skin beneath my hands. To finally experience the memories that kept me alive for three long, hellish, frustrating and devastating years."

Neck bent, straining toward her, waiting for the first sign she wanted the same thing, Evan watched a myriad of emotions flash through her eyes—longing, desperation, love.

But then they were gone, replaced by a blank stare that was worse than even her anger.

She brushed his hand away. "Well, what I want is to not have been lied to. To not have buried the last remaining person who mattered to me. I want to not have been left devastated and broken. So I guess we're both going to be disappointed."

2

GOD, SHE WANTED—desperately—to leave him to figure out how to get out of the cold night by himself.

But she couldn't do it. A heavy weight had settled right in the center of her chest, a ball of emotion and tears and hope and devastation.

Walking away should have made it better. Embracing the anger flickering through her should have given her the strength she needed to protect herself from getting hurt—again.

But less than three paces away from him, instead of relief flooding in, the pain and pressure had become worse.

Evan had lied to her. Or he'd let the government lie to her, let her believe he was dead. She didn't owe him a damn thing.

The Evan she knew was ruthless and resourceful. If he'd wanted to get in touch with her he would have.

Which should have made her angrier. Not sad.

The sob she'd been holding at bay clawed at the back of her throat. No. She wasn't letting it out.

Opening the driver's side door of her Mustang, she tipped the seat forward and shoved her bags into the backseat. Willow would kill her if she saw her crumpling the dress bag this way, but she didn't have the energy to worry about her friend's indignation.

Turning, she bent to slip inside, intent on pulling the door closed.

She would not look back at him. *She would not look back at him.*

The words rang through her head like a litany, but apparently her brain wasn't keen on actually following the instruction because her rebellious gaze strayed straight back to him.

Oh, Jesus.

And she almost doubled over at the pain lancing through her, an echo of the reaction she'd had when they'd told her he was dead. Why did learning he was alive hurt just as much?

Even across the space of the parking lot, she could feel the heat of his gaze as he watched her. The familiar tingle that blasted across her skin. The physical reaction only he had ever been able to coax from her body.

Damn the man.

His body was strung tight, arms heavy with muscle crossed over his wide chest as his dark gaze probed her. To anyone else who cared to look, he appeared relaxed, but she knew better. She could read the tension whipping through him.

Evan hadn't followed her, but she knew, instinctively, he wasn't giving up. Once her husband set his mind to something, he was relentless. Always had been, always would be.

Those qualities had served him well in his work for Special Ops. Once he took on a responsibility, he wouldn't back down or buckle under until the job was done.

It was always something she'd admired…until that dedication had killed him. Or, at least, she'd thought it had.

Her brain was scrambled. Her emotions bounced all over the place. She'd already been exhausted from a full few days of running Petals, arranging the flowers for the wedding and attending all the wedding activities before this mess had landed in her lap.

What she really wanted to do was go home, climb into a steaming tub of fragrant water and soak away all her cares.

But Evan had come here for a reason and she knew him well enough to realize he wouldn't leave until he'd accomplished whatever he'd set out to do.

The longer she dragged this out the harder it would be. A part of her wanted to thwart him simply to make him suffer. The rest of her realized that would be heaping punishment on her own head right along with his.

She was happy in Sweetheart. It had taken her months to find the equilibrium she'd lost. All she wanted was to return to the predictable, safe and easy life she'd built here.

Evan showing up threatened that stability. The sooner he left, the sooner her life could return to normal.

Besides, as much as she wanted to pretend it didn't matter, she needed answers. Maybe with closure, she'd finally be able to move on and find the happiness her friends had all discovered in the last few months.

Tatum realized she'd been staring at him for several minutes, half in and half out of her gaping car door. Long enough for delicate snowflakes to melt into her hair, dampening the ends. A chill seeped under her warm coat, although she wasn't sure it actually had anything to do with the weather.

The thought of letting Evan back into any part of her life sent panic skittering across her skin.

But she didn't have a better option.

Gripping the top of the door, she called, "Follow me," across the empty night before she could change her mind.

He didn't answer, although she really didn't give him a chance, slamming the door shut between them. Not that the empty symbolic gesture would save her.

He either followed or he didn't. Now the choice was his.

EVAN DROVE BEHIND the sleek, growling, piece of American machinery. It didn't surprise him to see that Tatum owned a vintage Mustang. That was his girl, always appreciative of the power and precision of a well-made car.

There had been a time, in their younger years, when she'd have opened it up, letting the car eat asphalt. They'd both loved the adrenaline rush of going fast. It was something they shared.

Whether it was the unpredictable weather and slick roads or something else, he wasn't sure, but tonight Tatum kept the car at a respectable pace as she led him through town, down a quaint little Main Street lined with shops and boutiques and into a neighborhood of cookie-cutter houses.

The entire town looked like a gingerbread house had thrown up all over it. Everywhere he looked, there were candy canes and blinking lights, wreaths and evergreen garlands strung with glittering tinsel.

It was idyllic. The kind of place that should be the setting for a made-for-TV movie about the magic of Christmas. The whole place made the spot right between his shoulder blades itch.

He wondered how Tatum felt about the obvious, in-your-face *peace on earth and goodwill toward men* theme Sweetheart had going.

This time of year had always been difficult for her. A reminder of everything that had gone wrong and all she'd lost. When they had been together, Evan had always gone out of his way to keep a smile on her face from Thanksgiving to Christmas. Leaving little notes and surprise gifts. Nothing fancy or expensive. Trinkets. Toys. Whatever would lighten her heart just a bit.

He wondered who was helping her keep the grief and guilt that she struggled with at bay.

Tatum turned into a driveway halfway down the street. The door for the garage rose and she maneuvered the Mustang inside. Without stopping to think about it, Evan pulled into the space beside her, which was mostly empty except for a row of plastic bins, a ladder and a mountain bike with a helmet hanging from one handlebar.

Kicking out the stand, he let the weight of his Harley settle beneath him as the engine went silent. Behind him, the garage door whirred shut, plunging them into a murky darkness that was alleviated only by the diffuse light of a single bulb above them.

Tatum sat in her car, hands gripping the steering wheel as she stared straight at the back wall of the garage. For a brief moment, he thought about walking around and pulling her out, but decided it was better to let her set the pace of this conversation.

It was going to be difficult enough.

Evan watched her shoulders rise and fall on a single, deep breath. Her eyes slid shut and the muscles along her shoulders tightened.

He wanted nothing more than to wrap her in his arms and promise her everything would be okay. But she'd made it very clear she didn't want him to touch her. Yet.

Although he wasn't entirely certain how long he would be able to deny the need roaring inside him. Three years was a damn long time, especially with drug kingpins constantly thrusting half-naked girls in his face.

He'd gotten a reputation as being cold and indifferent, ignoring all of the female flesh dangled as enticement.

The other men in the cartel had viewed his refusal as a sign of weakness, used it as an excuse to challenge his position within the organization. Even knowing it could cost him his life, he hadn't touched any of the women. That had been his line in the sand, because what good would living do him if he couldn't come home to Tatum with a clear conscience?

In the end, having to defend himself against the men who mistook his choice for vulnerability had worked in his favor, even if the price had been bloody and unpleasant. The moment he'd driven a seven-inch knife straight through another man's hand rather than be forced to lose his principles, his trajectory straight into the heart of the cartel had been assured.

No one questioned him again.

Unfortunately, he'd become something of a challenge to the women who tried to entice him. Not that he'd been tempted.

However, the desire that had lain dormant as scantily clad women paraded around in front of him reared up now to nearly choke him. A primitive, pounding need surged through him, a steady beat through his brain. His hands shook with the instinct to touch Tatum, hold her, finally reclaim her as his.

He needed to get a tight grip on his control or he was going to screw this up totally. He'd been around men who viewed women as commodities way too long, apparently. But at least he was smart enough to realize Tatum would not respond well to that kind of behavior.

Clenching his hands into fists, Evan set them on his thighs and waited.

She finally pushed from the car, juggling a couple of bags and her purse. The slap of her boots against the concrete floor echoed through the cold space of her quiet garage.

She bobbled her bags, shuffling everything around so she could insert her key into the lock. Evan shot forward, trying to take some of the burden from her arms, but she jerked everything out of his reach.

Pushing inside, she dumped it all onto a bench beside the door and kept going. The dress bag slithered to the floor in a heap. Tatum ignored it. Evan couldn't, reaching down to pick it up and fold it neatly back into place.

She continued through a small kitchen with a pile of dishes in the sink and into a den where she flicked on a single lamp. Warmth flooded the room and he knew immediately this was her sanctuary.

He also knew which chair was her favorite, could envision her curled up, feet tucked beneath her body and a heavy terra-cotta mug cradled between her hands as she stared sightlessly out the long window into the backyard, deep green eyes bleary as she waited for her first cup of coffee to kick in.

Tatum was not a morning person. But he'd always liked that about her. And had shamelessly taken advantage of that fact any chance he could, using her lethargy to convince her another hour in bed was a good idea...especially if they spent it together.

He hadn't realized the ghost of a smile played across his lips until the snap of Tatum's voice interrupted his thoughts.

"Stop smirking."

His gaze whipped to hers, the tug disappearing from his mouth. "I'm not."

Tatum stood behind a chocolate-brown sofa, her hands curled over the back as if it was the only lifeline keeping her safe.

"Oh, you were. I have no idea why, and I really don't care."

He didn't believe that for a minute. If he told her what had put that expression on his face she'd be spitting mad in seconds. Which might be an improvement from the wariness she watched him with now.

As though part of her expected him to leap across the sofa she'd placed between them and...ravish? Attack?

He had no idea what she thought, but obviously it was nothing good. At least, nothing she wanted.

Which only reinforced his own disquiet.

Could she sense just how far down the dark rabbit hole he'd had to go? That the trip had left marks on his soul he was deathly afraid could never be erased?

"So." Her single word hung in the air between them, an invitation he wasn't quite ready to accept. He knew she wanted answers. Deserved them. But…he wasn't certain what her reaction would be. He hesitated.

"So," he countered, his head tipping sideways. "You look good."

"Gee, thanks. So do you, for a ghost."

Inwardly, Evan cringed at the acid dripping from her words.

"Stop screwing around and just tell me whatever it is you've come to say."

His mouth went dry. His sharp eyes took in the way her knuckles had gone white where she gripped the sofa. They could both use a drink.

Shooting his gaze around the room, he was grateful to find exactly what he'd been looking for. Crossing the room to a buffet set against the far wall, he recognized the crystal bar set his Aunt Bethany had given them after their wedding.

Sitting next to it on a small table was the only homage to the upcoming holiday he'd seen—a small live tree no more than three feet tall and decorated entirely in gold, blue and chocolate ornaments. It was an afterthought. Expected, but not really wanted. And seeing it made his heart ache a little more.

Grabbing a bottle of Maker's Mark whiskey, he snagged two of the glasses and poured a healthy dose into each.

Walking back to her, Evan was careful to keep the sofa between them as he offered her one. Tatum's gaze dropped to the cut crystal and the amber liquid glittering in the bottom of it. She hesitated, and for a moment he thought she was going to refuse.

Her hand trembled as she wrapped it around the cool glass. The warmth of her fingers brushed his. The touch blasted straight through his body, burning in his belly almost as sharply as the drink he hadn't tasted yet.

His knees pressed against the sofa as his body leaned into the space between them. Tatum jerked away, whiskey sloshing over the side of her glass and dripping onto the cushions.

Her mouth opened. Heat flashed through her eyes. But she slammed it shut before any words fell out.

God, he desperately wanted to bridge the space between them, take her in his arms and kiss the hell out of her. He just wasn't certain the best way to do it.

It was the first time in their entire relationship that Evan had felt uncertain. Which only made his nerves worse. Turning his back on her and the uncomfortable sensation, he paced away.

"Everyone thought I was dead."

"No shit."

"No, I mean for weeks, everyone, the Army, my CO, those in charge of our joint operation, thought I'd died along with the rest of our team."

"But you didn't."

He faced her and his lips gave a sarcastic twitch, "Obviously. Our informant, a local who our contacts had been getting information from for eighteen months without any indication of a problem, gave the team up. I'm still not sure why, but after seeing how the cartel operated, I have a good idea."

But he wasn't going to tell her about the torture, kidnapping, blackmail and extortion he'd witnessed.

Evan slammed back his whiskey and immediately wanted another. Stalking over to the sideboard, he poured a finger, considered it for a moment and splashed a little more into the glass.

Glancing over his shoulder, he took in Tatum,

standing exactly where she'd been moments before, feet glued to the floor, drink untouched, wide eyes blank but watchful, trained straight on him.

"I shouldn't even be telling you this. The mission is still classified."

"The Army can kiss my ass."

"Ha," he grunted. Tatum had always understood the reasons why he couldn't share details of his job with her. She'd never pushed or complained. But he supposed, all things considered, some bitterness was to be expected.

"To preserve the illusion that none of us on the team knew each other, we came into the organization at different times and through different avenues. I was pulled in off the streets as a low-level drug dealer who was looking to climb the ranks and be useful. Two more guys received an introduction from our informant. Another used the sister of a mid-level enforcer and a fifth came in as a 'cousin' of one of their mules. I was the first one in and more than a week ahead of the others.

"The only time I encountered our informant was while I was under so he had no way of knowing I was part of the team. That's the only thing that saved my life that night."

As much as he fought against the memories, just the mention of the events caused ugly images to swirl inside his brain. Evan started to combat them with the alcohol in his hand, but realized what he was doing with it halfway to his mouth and reversed direction, slamming the glass to the table instead.

His skin crawled, not with bitterness and anger, but with frustration and restlessness. It was a familiar sensation, one he'd fought for three long, interminable years. How many nights had he lain in his crappy, filthy bed and fantasized about simply putting a bullet in several heads?

It would have been so easy. No way in hell he'd have made it out of the compound alive, but at least he would have gotten vengeance for his brothers. But he wasn't that man. Wouldn't let himself become that man.

Just as he hadn't drowned out the nasty memories with alcohol…or the abundance of drugs that had been at his fingertips. It would have been a quick release and relief. But he hadn't—although there were times when that resolve had been touch and go, the darkness yawning with the welcome invitation of reprieve.

He just needed to finish it. Explain to Tatum what had happened and that he'd never wanted to leave her—to let her think he was dead—and then figure out how to rebuild the life they'd once had.

Before he could get the words out, the ring of her doorbell cut him off. Tatum jumped, a tiny sound of surprise falling from her open lips. That moment of vulnerability didn't last long, though. Her jaw snapped shut.

An unhappy sigh blasted through her rigid lips, fluttering the fringe of her bangs. They were new. He liked them. They made her look a little more innocent than he knew she really was.

Setting her untouched glass onto a table, Tatum cut him a look before heading to the front door. He had no idea what that look was supposed to convey. Was she angry at him for the interruption?

Before she'd gotten the door open more than an inch, it was snatched out of her hands and forced inward. Obviously, neither of them had expected that reaction. Tatum jumped backward with a yelp. Evan reached to the small of his back for a firearm that wasn't where it should be and cursed. He was already halfway across the room, ready to yank her behind the protective wall of his body when the high-pitched sound of several female voices hit his ears.

"Ohmygod, Tatum, are you okay? Willow told us what happened outside the church. We texted to see if you needed anything."

"We were going to wait until morning to come by, but when you didn't respond…"

"We got worried…"

The women ran over each other, one sentence blending seamlessly into the next as if they were one person instead of three speaking.

"Why the hell didn't you tell us you were married? I wouldn't have tried so hard to set you up with my cousin Matt."

"Because *that's* why you should have kept Matt away from her, not because he's a pretentious jerk."

The three women rushed inside Tatum's house. They were all clad in the same dress she'd been wearing not an hour ago. A blonde with amazing curves reached for Tatum, setting hands on her shoulders and peering intently into her eyes. "Seriously, are you okay?"

The tall, thin brunette she'd been with earlier reached around them both, running a hand softly down Tatum's arm to grasp her hand. "What do you need?"

The other woman pressed in tight, forming a protective knot of femininity with Tatum in the center. Evan fought the urge to wade through them all and pull her out. He didn't know any of these people and didn't like having them stand between him and his wife.

Behind the commotion, two men in dark suits hovered. They moved slower, quietly closed the door and stood to the side, observing in a way that told him they were used to these kinds of female displays of excitement and solidarity. He saw acceptance tinged with exasperation and a little bafflement.

None of the women had noticed him yet, but the men sized him up as soon as they walked in.

With silent agreement, they scooted around the cluster of women to present a wall of male power that had his hands preemptively tightening into fists. Instinct drove him to counter with his own display, but something told him Tatum wouldn't appreciate a testosterone-fueled show.

Frustration kicked through his stomach, but he clamped down hard on it. Lots of practice at that.

"I'm assuming you're her husband," the darker of the two men said softly. There was something about him that Evan recognized, appreciated. A dangerous edge that told him he could take care of his own if needed.

The other guy was a bit bigger, but not by much. He seemed...softer wasn't the right word because neither of them were teddy bears. He didn't have quite the same edge as the other man, although Evan wouldn't want to meet either of them in a dark alley alone.

Not that he couldn't take them—together if necessary.

"Evan Huntley," he said, stepping forward and offering his hand.

Neither of them took it. They simply stared at him.

The female chatter behind them screeched to a halt. Several pairs of eyes peered around the wall of masculinity, including Tatum's wide, unhappy green eyes.

"Oh shit," one of the women breathed.

"You've got that right," another agreed.

"Tatum never mentioned she had a husband," the bigger guy said, his wide mouth pulled down into a deep frown.

Evan realized what the man was fishing for was an explanation, but considering he hadn't even given the whole thing to Tatum yet he wasn't about to spill to a stranger—several strangers.

"Willow said you were dead. Supposed to be dead."

An unhappy smile tugged at the edges of his lips. "Which would explain why Tatum never mentioned me."

The curvy blonde poked her head around the tall guy, laying a hand on his arm in a comfortable, possessive gesture that immediately told him they were together. "Not really."

He pinned his wife with a sharp gaze. "I'm sure she had her reasons for not telling you about her past." All eyes swung around to her. Any other woman might have squirmed beneath the weight of that scrutiny, but not Tatum. She kept her expression bland and stared back, mouth shut and spine straight.

Apparently realizing they weren't getting anywhere with her, the focus quickly returned to him.

He'd faced down terrorists, murderers, drug dealers and rapists—singly and in groups larger than this one. But for some reason, his palms began to sweat and a cold trickle of unease whispered down his spine.

Not because he honestly thought they'd do him any harm, but because he was afraid their opinion could sway Tatum, and without knowing anything about them, he couldn't begin to guess their response to the messy affair.

Shaking her head, Tatum pushed between the two

guys. "While I appreciate the chivalry act, I don't need it. Willow, Lexi, can you please control your men?"

The blonde snorted. "Fat chance."

Maybe it was time he offered something. "Let me assure everyone Tatum has nothing to fear from me. I'm not here to hurt her."

Willow frowned. "You already have."

3

TATUM WAS EXHAUSTED, mentally and physically. It had taken quite a while to convince the cavalry she'd be fine with Evan and get them to finally leave. By then it was after midnight and all she wanted was a soft pair of pajamas and her warm bed.

Yes, she still had questions—plenty of them—but just from the little he'd already told her, it was obvious she was going to need a clear head for the answers.

It was awkward, setting Evan up in her guest bedroom, but no matter how he looked at her, she wasn't letting him back in *her* bed. Certainly not until they talked. And probably not even then.

He was different. Harder, colder, though she had seen flashes of the honorable, dedicated man she'd fallen in love with at seventeen underneath the new layers. Sighing, Tatum supposed she was different, as well. They were both evidence that a lot could happen in three years.

Deciding their conversation was probably better saved for the morning when her brain would be less fuzzy, she'd convinced him to wait. The sharp set of his mouth had broadcast just how unhappy he'd been about her decision, but at least he hadn't argued.

Tatum slipped beneath the sheets, fully expecting to drop right to sleep. Exhaustion pulled at her muscles, but her brain wouldn't shut up. Thoughts, possibilities and fears, spun like an EF-5 tornado, shredding her composure and leaving her just as devastated as any broken landscape.

Maybe she should have just gotten it over with.

Too late now. No doubt Evan was fast asleep. He'd always been the kind of guy who was out the moment his head hit a pillow, and that skill set had only become more pronounced when he had joined Special Ops.

What was she going to do?

She had no idea. Conflicting wants tore her apart— crawling beside him and wrapping her arms around his big, hard body just so she could assure herself he really was alive warred with yanking him up out of her guest bed and shoving him quickly out the front door.

An hour later, Tatum was still staring at the pattern of shadows playing across her ceiling when a loud whimper crashed into the silent night.

Her body responded, an old habit, as she bounded up from the bed. Her naked feet hit the cold hardwood floor, but she barely registered the winter chill seeping into her.

It wasn't the first time she'd woken to Evan's nightmares. He'd been having them as long as she knew him, leftovers from a childhood that had been less than ideal. Their crappy history was something they'd shared.

But as she ran into the room next door, one look was all she needed to realize this was something more.

He wasn't thrashing around under the covers, eyes closed and ragged sounds falling through half-parted lips.

Evan's gorgeous hazel eyes, more brown than green, were wide open, but completely unfocused. He crouched in the corner of the room, his back pressed tight against the wall. If she hadn't heard the unintelligible words pouring from his mouth in harsh whispers, she might not have seen him in the shadows. He'd found the darkest spot in the room, and with his black hair, tanned skin and stubble-covered jaw, he nearly blended in. She could just make out the heavy lines of the tattoos covering his chest and ribs in the gloom.

Tatum's heart clenched at the sight of him. It was wrong to see such a strong, noble man hunkered down in the corner as if defending his very life.

Uncertainty froze her limbs. The harsh sound of his breathing finally galvanized her into motion. She had to do *something*.

With measured steps, she moved closer, her hands lifted up, palms out to show she meant no harm.

"Evan," she said cautiously. "Sweetheart." The word she hadn't said for so long felt foreign in her mouth. "You're fine. You're safe."

Stopping several feet away, Tatum crouched in front of him, hoping to catch his gaze. But when she did, she realized he was still…asleep. Or caught up in whatever nightmare had ripped into him. Definitely not focused on the here and now.

She shifted, and the world exploded. Or at least it felt that way.

Suddenly, she was on her back, her head cracking against the hard floor, her left shoulder colliding with the edge of the dresser. And all of Evan's weight drove against her, pushing oxygen from her body.

She let out a soft cry with whatever breath she had left.

His hands dug into her muscles, pinning her in place. Leaning down, he growled into her ear. She realized he wasn't speaking gibberish, but another language she didn't understand.

She didn't need to know the words to realize whatever he was saying wasn't nice. His menacing tone was more than enough.

The pain that had exploded through her body on impact faded. Tears sprang to her eyes, not from that, but from the realization that there was so much she didn't know…or understand. Gripping his waist, for the first time in three years, Tatum felt the soft slide of his skin against her fingertips. Need, lust and love exploded through her, a potent combination she didn't have room for right now.

Pushing her body's reaction away, she smoothed her hands up his ribs, over his chest to cup his face.

"Evan," she whispered, pulling him down even as she rose to brush her lips across his mouth in a butterfly kiss.

What she'd meant to be something soothing quickly burst into fully involved flame.

His mouth devoured hers, all hunger and heat and demand. She was helpless to fight off her response to him. His wide palms settled, one at her hip, the other at the curve of her neck, arching her closer. He immobilized her beneath him, the hard length of his body holding her prisoner.

Not that she wanted free. She wanted more. Even as her brain screamed at her to stop, her body simply melted, turning gooey as a marshmallow introduced to heat.

His tongue swept into her mouth, tangling, stroking, teasing. He crowded against her, giving her no place to go, nothing to counter the drowning need.

God, she'd missed this. Missed him. So damn much. No man had ever made her feel the way Evan did. Desired. Alive. Protected. Cherished.

The combination was addictive. And always had been.

But she wasn't a seventeen-year-old kid anymore.

His hips, clad in loose-fitting sweats, slid against hers, pumping in a slow and deliberate way that caused liquid heat to pool in the center of her body. The length of his erection, caught between them, ground into her, making her own hips pulse in quick, pleading jerks.

What was wrong with her? Where had her resolve gone? At the first touch of his strong body against hers, she was crumbling like an ancient ruin.

Tatum knew the exact moment Evan came back to himself. Pressed so closely together, she felt the jolt of awareness as it slammed into him.

Before she could blink, he ripped away from her. His back collided with the wall, the room practically shaking from the impact. From her vantage point on the floor, she could see long red welts forming across his skin where her nails had torn through him. He didn't seem to notice the pain that must have come with the scratches.

Horrified, he stared at her for several seconds before finally sliding down the wall. Burying his face in two wide, rough palms, he whispered, "Jesus."

The sound of the single, broken word sent regret,

pain and fear tumbling through her. What the hell had he lived through?

Finally looking up, he peered at her out of hard, dead eyes that did more to scare her than being flung unceremoniously onto her back. "Leave. Now, Tatum."

And that pissed her off.

"No, Evan. This is my house, my guest room. I'm not going anywhere."

For the second time tonight, his big body exploded outward in a flurry of movement and muscle. He tore away from the wall, stalking toward her with a menace that was clearly meant to intimidate. And it had probably been very effective on his enemies, but Tatum knew Evan. Possibly better than he knew himself.

Or she used to.

But she trusted her instincts, which were telling her he'd hurt himself before he'd ever hurt her.

At least, physically.

She swallowed. The confidence she'd been shoring up wavered as he got closer. Reaching down, he wrapped heavy hands around her biceps and pulled her up from the floor. His hold didn't hurt, but it wasn't soft and easy, either.

He set her on her feet, but didn't back away. Instead, he continued to press into her personal space, leaving her off-kilter in the way only Evan could.

"Don't ever do that again. I could have seriously injured you," he said, his voice full of gravel and self-recrimination.

"You didn't."

He snorted, the sound grating. Before she could stop him, his hands speared into her hair, tumbling the strands from the messy knot she'd piled at the crown of her head. He rubbed around the curve of her skull, giving her an "I told you so" look when she couldn't stop the sharp intake of breath as he found a tender spot.

But he didn't stop there. Spinning her, he pushed the thin strap on the gown she'd worn to bed off her shoulder and down her arm. Her skin was exposed and she was half-naked before she realized what he was doing.

Cold air brushed across her bared breast and her nipple tightened. Her knees buckled. Why wouldn't they? Her body was still burning from that damn kiss. If he hadn't been holding on to her waist, she probably would have collapsed to the floor again.

But Evan was too busy at her shoulder to notice.

Dragging in a breath, Tatum tried to steady her response, get control of her body.

He might have torn at her clothes like a madman, but his touch was gossamer soft and utterly careful. She could barely feel the roughened pads of his fingertips as they smoothed across her shoulder, down the ridge of her scapula and onto the first swell of her ribs.

Goose bumps erupted across her skin. Her nervous system hadn't gotten the memo that this wasn't supposed to be a seduction.

He probed, paying special attention to one area that smarted.

Tatum closed her eyes at the unbelievable sensation of him touching her. That kiss, he hadn't been all there. Tatum knew he'd still been cloudy from whatever nightmare had gripped him and not completely in control of his actions.

He was definitely clearheaded now.

How many times over the last few years had she fantasized about this exact thing? Wished, prayed, begged for one more night with him? A night of caresses and kisses and feeling him move deep inside her.

One more night of the connection she'd only ever found with him.

She'd finally gotten her wish, but she was afraid it was three years too late.

"I don't think anything's seriously damaged," he said, "but you're going to have a couple of nasty bruises in the morning."

Crossing an arm to hide her chest, Tatum craned her neck so she could see him. He stared at her shoulder, completely oblivious to the fact that he'd bared her breast without thinking.

Well, if that didn't burst a girl's bubble, Tatum wasn't certain what would.

"It's fine. I won't break. I'm tougher than I look."

His gaze dragged up to hers. He was so close there was no way she could miss the expressions swirling through his haunted eyes—regret, anger, acceptance and, finally, desire.

That single flare of heat blasted through her body, scorching her along the way.

Okay, he did still want her.

Tatum wasn't sure that was a good thing.

His touch changed, no longer assessing, but with an edge of worship that would be hard for any woman to ignore. As if he'd never felt anything better than the texture of her skin. As if he could stand there, doing nothing but touch her for hours and be perfectly content. As if he couldn't get enough.

Tatum's pulse fluttered. Her lips parted and she swiped her tongue across the suddenly dry surface.

Evan's gaze traveled down her body, taking in the disheveled state of her gown. His fingers dragged across the tiny strap now hanging below her elbow.

She wanted him to take it off. Instead, he gently tugged it back into place. His index finger glided over the ridge of material from her back, over her shoulder and down onto her chest. Her body arched, an involuntary motion that tried to get him close to the aching tip of her breast. But he ignored the offer.

Instead, he stepped back, the chill of the winter night blasting through her.

"I'm sorry," he whispered, and then darted from the room, snatching up the shirt he'd draped across a chair.

The reverberation of her front door slamming shut had barely faded before the angry roar of his bike kicked up outside.

Tatum swayed in the middle of her guest bedroom, heart pounding, pulse thrumming, pain, fear, hope and need mixing into a toxic sludge in her belly as she listened to the sound of him leaving.

Would he be back?

Did she want him to come back?

Or would it be better for both of them if he just… disappeared and left her to the life she'd built without him?

HE COULDN'T REMEMBER the dream, not that it really mattered. Take your pick, he had several, all running with the same theme—blood, nasty behavior and killer choices. Holding a gun to a man's head and trying desperately to figure out how to keep him alive without blowing his own cover and getting himself killed in the process. Handing drugs to a ten-year-old kid who was just trying to make enough money to care for his mom and sisters in the only way he knew how, when what Evan had really wanted to do was whisk him away from the dangerous life before he got in too deep.

But he hadn't been able to save the boy. Or his fellow soldiers. He'd watched them all die and had been given one chance for survival.

What really bothered him about tonight was that he could have seriously hurt Tatum. Easily. And it wouldn't have been anything he hadn't already done, while defending himself against the scum he'd been wallowing with for the last three years. He'd quickly moved up the ranks of the cartel, which had made walking that thin line between right and wrong more difficult—and the target on his back even bigger.

It was mere luck that had prevented Tatum from getting a concussion, a knife to the throat or a bullet in the brain. In Colombia, Evan had slept with a gun under his pillow, finger already lodged on the trigger, and a knife strapped to his thigh. Just in case.

Days earlier, he had, with difficulty, given up the knife and gun—the two things that had made him feel safe in an environment he had little control over. But he had realized part of coming home was assimilating back into the real world. He no longer lived in the dirty, depraved underworld.

But he'd been immersed in it for so long he wasn't sure he'd ever get the stench off his skin.

Revving his bike, Evan pushed it a little harder, thrilling to the purr of the powerful motor between his thighs. The sensation did little to assuage the hard-on he'd been sporting since the moment Tatum had walked out of that damn church.

He wanted her. Needed her. With a desperation that was almost as alarming as coming to with her pinned beneath his body, his fingers digging into her tender flesh while he practically violated her.

Hell, he'd been grinding against her like a teenager intent on dry-humping his way to heaven. And kissing her so hard he was surprised the inside of her mouth wasn't shredded.

Despite the chilly temperatures, a cold sweat broke out across his forehead. God, one night back with her and he'd almost hurt her. Maybe his CO was right and he should have taken some more time to decompress before returning.

But after three, long, miserable years, it had seemed as though seeing her, touching her, feeling her was the only thing that could convince him the nightmare was finally over.

And that there was still a square inch of his soul that hadn't rotted away with the rest beneath the weight of the things he'd done to survive and complete the mission.

Tatum was holding back. He could feel the walls she put up between them. Walls that had never been there before. But he supposed he couldn't blame her.

The problem was, he wasn't entirely certain how to rip them down…at least not without ripping *her*, too. But he would figure it out. He had to. He needed her to survive.

With the same tenacity and will that had kept him alive when everyone around him was dying, he would find a way to get what he wanted. A way back into her life, her heart and her bed, although he was hoping not necessarily in that order.

The cell phone at his hip buzzed. It was late, or early depending on your definition, and only a handful of people knew his number—none of whom he actually wanted to talk to. But the fact that they were bothering him at all couldn't be good, especially at this hour.

Pulling over into a small park, Evan kicked out the stand and flung his leg over the chrome and black monster. Moonlight poured across the empty slide and silent merry-go-round. The chains on the swings creaked as a winter breeze blew them gently back and forth, like the ghosts of children past were getting one last ride.

The sight was eerie, but somehow also hopeful. He couldn't remember the last time he'd seen a playground. And there was no doubt in his mind that in just a few hours this one would be full of laughing, happy children despite the bleak weather.

His phone had stopped vibrating before he could answer, but he knew it would probably start up again any second. Stalking across the park, Evan plopped down into one of the swings and waited.

And he wasn't wrong. The phone rattled against his hip. He didn't bother to look at the display before answering, "Huntley."

"Buddy," came the low, gruff reply. "Just wanted to see how your first night back in the real world went."

There was a time in Evan's life when Locklyn Granger had been a buddy. They'd trained together, served together, had each other's backs on more occasions than Evan could count. They'd shared even more beers and had a few rambunctious stories—Locklyn's not his. Evan was always the observer.

But it was difficult to find the same easy camaraderie they'd shared before. It wasn't that Evan didn't trust him anymore…it was that he didn't trust anyone. Too many years of being alone and constantly circled by angry, hungry wolves looking for a reason to drag him down.

It didn't help that the man was obviously lying to him.

"So you called at—" Evan rolled his wrist to look at the expensive multitasking watch that also happened to tell time "—one-thirty in the morning to see how my day went? I call bullshit, Lock. What's really going on?"

The heavy sigh at the other end of the line didn't do anything to help temper the sudden kick of adrenaline through Evan's heart.

"Nothing. Probably nothing. Just some chatter that came through some reputable channels. Nothing specific or actionable."

"But enough for you to pick up the phone and wake me up if I'd been asleep."

Lock snorted, the sound hard and sharp. "Please. I've been there, man. Days after returning from what you went through, you're gonna be lucky to get three hours in a row. Chances were good you'd be awake."

He wasn't wrong. And it should have helped center Evan to realize he wasn't the only guy who'd ever suffered ill effects from a mission.

But it didn't.

As far as he was aware, Locklyn hadn't been read in on all the details, so the man had no freakin' clue what Evan had been through the last three years. And he had no intention of changing that status quo.

"So, what's the intel?"

"The Carbrera Cartel is scrambling."

Satisfaction rumbled through Evan's gut. They were scrambling because he'd taken down almost everyone who held any power, pretty much wiping the entire organization off the map. They could attempt to recover, but it would take a lot of time and money to put their network back into play. Time in which drugs wouldn't be flooding onto American streets.

"Good."

"Yeah." Evan heard the appreciation and pride in the

other man's voice. "Not unexpected, but the chatter is a little more organized than we'd anticipated."

"What do you mean?"

"We think they already have someone ready to pick up the reins."

Evan jerked from the swing and began pacing. His feet crunched on the frozen ground as he stomped back and forth in front of the groaning swings. His mind raced, mentally flipping through pictures of men who could possibly step into the leadership role of a major drug organization.

There was no one.

He'd painstakingly assembled the evidence to bring down the entire damn organizational structure. That's why he had been away for three shitty years. It had taken him time to work his way up to the point where he'd been privy to useful information. He could have turned over one or two guys a year into the assignment and come home earlier.

And the year—and the men he'd lost—would have been useless because those vacancies would have immediately been filled by the next guy down the ladder. So he'd worked hard to build a web that would ensnare everyone and leave the organization floundering, hopefully enough to wither away and die.

Evan supposed someone from another organization could have stepped up to the plate, but the Carbreras weren't exactly known to play well with others. They had more enemies than options within the other crime syndicates, plenty of people wanted to see them disappear almost as much as the United States government had.

Evan swore under his breath. "Who?"

"We don't know. We were hoping you'd tell us."

Evan tipped his head up to the bright sky drenched with moonlight. The stars were gorgeous, so crisp and clear. Not the way they were back home in Detroit, overshadowed by clusters of lights. Maybe that's what Tatum liked about this place. It was definitely quieter. Calmer.

Calm was good. He could use calm right now, because Lock's words had dread cramping hard in his belly.

"I have no idea who it is."

Would this nightmare never be over?

4

HE HADN'T COME BACK, at least not by the time Tatum left for work the next morning. She wasn't sure how to feel—pissed, relieved, disappointed. Some combination that had her thoughts scattered and her fingers fumbling as she tried to put together bouquets and fill orders.

Normally she was closed on Sundays, but because of the wedding, she'd let a few things slide. Her display case was looking pitiful and desperately empty. She hadn't made a bank deposit in three days, and if she didn't place an order for flowers from the wholesaler soon, she wasn't going to have any inventory to sell.

She tried not to make a habit of coming in on Sundays, but there was something soothing about it—no interruptions from the phone or front door. No lost delivery drivers to deal with or shipments with broken stems.

Well, it was *usually* soothing. Today the quiet made the thoughts revving through her brain race louder.

Grasping a heavy vase full of cream roses, stargazer lilies, snapdragons and salal, Tatum pushed through the door separating her work area from the retail space, but stopped dead in her tracks halfway to the large stand-ing cooler.

Outside, Evan leaned against the large plate-glass window at the front of her store. The *S* of Petals ap-peared to curve around his body, almost hugging his hips. Rose petals at the bottom of her logo scattered across the window, large to small, until they faded away into nothing. The evergreen garland she'd hung under the eaves trailed above his head.

His back was to her, his body easy and loose, as if he could wait there all day. She didn't doubt it; the man had the patience of Job. It had often irritated her, how he could wait out her temper whenever she'd gotten angry.

In the past, she'd been quick to flare and quicker to cool down. Staying angry with him had never been her strong suit.

Not that she was going to fall back into bad pat-terns. Not this time. This wasn't him forgetting to call her while he was out playing wingman for Lock. Or trading in his car for a Harley without talking to her about it first.

Taking a deep breath, Tatum finished her trip to the cooler and set the arrangement on the shelf.

The sooner they got this over with…

Cold air swirled in when she flipped the lock and opened the door for him. He didn't say anything, just straightened from his slouched position and sauntered inside.

Irritation bubbled through her veins. Which was good. She needed it, especially after last night. Oth-erwise, she was liable to flash back to that damn kiss.

He brushed close to her body. Her nipples tight-ened. She told herself it was the cold, but she knew that was a lie.

After busying herself with locking up behind him, Tatum bustled into the back and trusted he'd follow.

"Nice to know you're not in a broken heap on the side of the road," she threw over her shoulder. The door started to swing shut in his face, but he caught it, the smack of his hands against wood reverberating between them.

"Nice to know you care."

"Who said I do? You roared off so hot and bothered, any decent human being would be worried. Especially when you didn't come back."

And that was another lie—of course she cared. At first, she'd been angry. Obviously. Then she'd gotten worried. And started imagining his body a contorted pile on the side of the highway somewhere.

It had done a number on her head. If he'd died the day he popped back into her life…she might have hired some black magician to raise him from the dead so she could strangle him herself.

Needless to say, she hadn't slept well.

Tatum reached for another handful of blooms, needing to keep her hands busy. She wasn't going to ask. She didn't want to know. It was none of her business. And yet, the words tumbled out anyway. "Where did you stay last night?"

"At that park in the middle of town."

A rose fell from her hands, bruising its velvety petals as it hit the table. "Dammit," she muttered under her breath, snatching up the flower to inspect it. "What do you mean you stayed at the park? It was freezing last night."

"I didn't notice."

Tatum stared at him. Did he have a death wish? Was that it? Or were the pain receptors in his brain not working? Sure, he'd always run a little hot, her own personal space heater during cold winters, but that was taking things to the extreme.

"Had things on my mind."

"What things?"

"Nothing for you to worry about."

A muffled sound of frustration rumbled through her chest. "Whatever." His secrets had never bothered her before. Probably since he'd always been open about what he could and couldn't tell her. It wasn't like he was lying to her…simply unable to give her all the details.

Now, though, those secrets had taken him from her, so maybe she was resentful.

"We need to finish our conversation."

Tatum dropped her focus to the flowers spread across her table. Something bright and cheerful, that's what she'd do next. Completely the opposite of the traditional Christmas green and red that always made her stomach feel as though a pit had opened up and was trying to swallow her insides. Something that would take her mind off whatever revelations and nightmares Evan was about to share.

Pulling out sunflowers, orange lilies, pink-tipped yellow roses, pink stock and alstroemeria, she placed the blooms together. "So start talking."

He heaved a sigh, but Tatum ignored it, keeping her hands moving as she fussed.

"Fine." He leaned against the table. "For weeks, everyone was under scrutiny as the cartel looked for more agents, moles or informants within their ranks. That first night was the bloodiest, but more of their own men died in the following days, and I was constantly worried I'd be next, especially since I no longer had any backup on the inside. But eventually, I started to think my cover would hold. Several more weeks passed before I realized everyone on the outside thought I was dead. By the time it was safe for me to make contact, you'd already buried me, Tatum."

"Uh-huh," she muttered, her brain spinning. Her imagination had always been decent. She could practically see the dark, shady buildings. The blood of his friends spreading across dirty concrete floors. Taste the fear he must have fought on a daily basis.

But those things didn't combat her bone-deep grief. Or the fact he had let her keep living with it.

"Dammit, Tatum, look at me!" His voice exploded through her. Unwanted tears pricked her eyes.

She refused, didn't want him to see her weakness. She picked up a rose and started stripping thorns.

Evan grasped her shoulders and, with unrelenting pressure, forced her to turn to him.

Her fist tightened around the stem. A thorn pricked her skin, drawing a gasp and giving her an excuse for the unshed tears swimming in her eyes.

Evan swore beneath his breath, pried her fingers away from the rose and threw it onto the table. A single dot of blood welled in the center of her palm.

Tatum was almost transfixed by the deep red color, just like the truest red rose.

Cupping her hand in his, Evan stretched out her arm even as he flipped on the faucet in the nearby sink and thrust her hand beneath the cool stream. Her skin stung as water mixed with blood. He kept her hand there until the reddish pink streak disappeared and ran clear.

After a few seconds, he slammed the water off

again, cradling her hand in his. Water dripped into the stainless sink, the only sound between them.

Evan's head bent. She had no idea what he was doing until his lips pressed softly against her skin.

This time, the gasp that erupted from her lips felt as though it was dragged from the center of her soul. Her body convulsed at the contact and the shivers only got worse as the warmth of his mouth rushed through her.

It stung—not the cut, but the sensation of his mouth on her. Like the pins and needles sensation of a limb waking up after the circulation is cut off for too long.

Jerking away, she tried to close her fist, but he wouldn't let her go. Straightening, Evan stared into her face. His hazel eyes had gone a tempting caramel brown, the way they always did when he wanted her. The memory of him looking at her with that same expression as he slowly slid inside her was more than she could handle.

"Let me go," she breathed.

"I can't."

She didn't think he was talking about her hand, but then maybe she hadn't been, either.

"I can't do this, Evan. You lied to me. Let me think you were dead."

"Every day that was a possibility, Tatum. I didn't want to give you hope only to have it snatched away from you days or months later. What I was doing was extremely dangerous. I watched men be murdered for the smallest of offenses. I could have died at any moment, even without them discovering I was with the US government."

"So you decided it was better to let me think you were dead."

His thumb stroked the inside of her wrist. She could

feel the thump of her own pulse against that tender, relentless, maddening motion.

The ever-present heat of him slipped out to envelope her. His scent—spicy, dangerous and tempting—somehow managed to overpower the flowers that surrounded them, making her dizzy and lightheaded.

"You were wrong," she whispered. "I'd have taken those few days or months of hope. You have no idea how much I needed it. You should have let them tell me, Evan. Then maybe there'd be a chance I could forgive you. That we could start again."

This time when she jerked back, he let her hand go. It dropped beside her, dead weight, although the inside of her wrist continued to tingle.

Somehow she found the strength to say, "I want you to leave, Evan."

He took a single step away. And then another. Panic climbed up the back of her throat, but she forced it down. She was making the right decision.

She followed him to the front door, keeping a steady space between them. Without looking, he flipped the lock open. The cheerful bell tinkled, rolling through her head in a wave of pain that was worse than any migraine.

"I'm not going anywhere, Tatum. You might not want to forgive me, but we both know I can wait you out. I have three years of practice being extremely patient."

BEING PATIENT MIGHT not be a problem, but being stupid apparently was. He'd walked out of her shop without a key to her house or another place to stay. Standing on the sidewalk outside the only hotel in town, he grimaced—the little old lady running the place had said there were no rooms available until Tuesday.

Beautiful.

"Evan, right?" A soft voice broke into his grim thoughts.

Looking to the right, he took in the tall, thin brunette staring at him, a frown tugging between her eyes.

One of the women from last night. Willow? He thought that's what Tatum had called her. The name fit. Even bundled up against the cold, she had an ethereal air that somehow managed not to clash with the edge of sophistication her obviously expensive clothes conveyed.

"Yeah. Willow?"

She nodded, continuing to study him. He wondered what this woman thought of him. What did she see? The hardened criminal he'd pretended to be for three long years? The husband desperate to find a way back to the life he was seriously starting to fear didn't exist anymore? A man who, for years, had been certain of his place and purpose, now floundering beneath the weight of choices he wasn't yet ready to make?

Or just the guy who'd made her friend gasp with surprise and pain?

"What are you doing out here?"

"Trying to decide how to grovel so Tatum will let me stay with her for a few days. I kinda stuck my foot in my mouth before checking to make sure the B and B had room."

Willow's mouth twitched with suppressed laughter, but she couldn't quite stop the twinkle glinting in her dark eyes.

He groaned. "Just guessing, but I figure flowers aren't the way to go."

"I wouldn't think so," she said, the cadence of her words a little too smooth. She was laughing at him. He supposed he deserved that.

"You guys seem pretty close. Any suggestions?"

"Why should I help you?"

"Because I've loved her since we were seventeen. Before that, actually. That was just when I was finally smart enough to realize the girl who'd always been a part of my life was growing into the kind of woman a man would die for."

At his words, the twinkle died. "Well, shit. How am I supposed to stay upset with you when you say things like that?"

It was Evan's turn to hold back a smile. "You aren't."

He'd seen the way her friends had rallied around Tatum. He figured he would need to convince them he wasn't a threat to her happiness. And maybe, just maybe, if he was lucky, he'd be able to cajole them into helping him.

Willow seemed a good a place to start. She struck him as fairly levelheaded.

"You let her think you were dead," she said.

"I had good reason. I wouldn't have done it if I didn't think it was the right thing to do—*for her*. I can't tell you the details. Hell, I'm not even supposed to tell her the details, but I will because she deserves them."

"Tatum has a temper."

"You're not telling me anything I don't already know. I actually like her temper. When we were younger, one of my favorite things was riling her up just to watch her spin. Makeup sex was always spectacular."

Willow made a choking sound deep in the back of

her throat. "Something tells me stellar sex isn't going to solve things for you this time."

No, but it certainly couldn't hurt. To remind Tatum just how amazing they were together. To rekindle their physical connection in the hope that the emotional ties would snap back into place, stronger now for being tested.

"Well," Willow said. "there's always Sugar and Spice. You can't go wrong with tempting any woman with chocolate."

He nodded. "Not a bad idea."

"And wine."

A little pampering. He'd show up tonight with dinner, wine and dessert.

"Just…take my advice and stay away from the aphrodisiac truffles."

"Aphrodisiac truffles?"

"Yeah, Lexi's specialty is herb-infused truffles guaranteed to rev up anyone's libido."

This had serious potential.

Evan had never been above playing dirty. He'd take whatever advantages came his way. He wanted to touch and taste and hold his wife. He needed the connection.

And something told him she did, as well.

It HAD BEEN a strange day. Tasks that should have taken her no time to complete took hours. Or maybe she was just dragging her feet. She didn't want to go home. Which was silly and stupid.

Evan wasn't there. And she'd lived in her house alone for a little over two years. She loved the space she'd built for herself, even if on occasion it had been too quiet.

There were days—not many, but they were there—when she missed the noise and frenzy of the city. Nights when the still silence roared in her ears louder than any street sounds.

Today was one of those days. To make matters worse, the blinking lights and brightly painted Christmas decorations were rubbing her the wrong way.

This time of year was always difficult for her. That first Thanksgiving after her mother died had been excruciating. She'd worked so damn hard to make the day special for her dad…tried to fill in the gap her mom had left. She'd slaved over a turkey and all the trimmings, pulling out her mom's old recipe cards for the traditional dishes they'd always enjoyed.

But by the time dinner had been ready, her father had been too drunk to eat anything. In the end, she'd sat alone at the table pushing turkey through puddles of brown gravy and mashed potatoes.

She'd probably have done it all over again for Christmas, but she hadn't gotten the chance.

According to the note he'd left, the looming loneliness of the holidays had been too much for him to fight against. Her dad had killed himself—stuck a pistol in his mouth and pulled the trigger—a couple of weeks later.

She'd walked in after work to find him lying on the living room floor, the lights from the tree she'd decorated days before blinking lazily, spilling color across his body and the sticky pool of blood spread beneath him.

God, the blood.

That was what she remembered every time she saw Christmas red. Not Santa or Rudolph or poinsettias.

She realized Evan's return at this already difficult

time of year was probably amplifying her reactions. But knowing it and being able to do something about it were two different things.

She was pissed at Evan for leaving the shop. It didn't matter she'd been the one to tell him to go. Emotions were hardly logical.

Changing out of the jeans and long-sleeved T-shirt she'd worn to Petals and into her softest pair of yoga pants and warmest pair of fuzzy socks, Tatum wandered into her kitchen and surveyed the granite counters, stainless appliances and sunny yellow cabinets.

She wasn't hungry. Hadn't been all day.

She padded to the den and flipped on the TV. It had been a while since she'd given herself an evening just to veg out and watch mindless shows. Maybe there'd be an *Ancient Aliens* marathon or some program about uncovering long lost civilizations.

She channel surfed, unable to find anything that caught her attention long enough to make her settle. It was one of the perks of living alone: she could watch five minutes of a show before abandoning it for something else.

Finally deciding on a rerun of *The Big Bang Theory*, she tossed the remote onto the sofa beside her and slumped against the cushions. She hadn't slept well last night. Who would, under the circumstances? She'd probably fall asleep and wake up in the middle of the night with a crick in her neck. But it was too early to head to bed, so...

The guys on television were arguing about some theory she didn't understand when her doorbell broke through her uneasy solitude. It was probably one—or all—of the girls. Now that she thought about it, she was surprised none of them had stopped by the shop today. Maybe they thought she'd be busy dealing with her resurrected husband.

A rough sound scraped through the back of her throat.

Shaking her head, she pushed up from the couch and trudged to the door. She wasn't up for their fussing tonight, but had no illusions she would be able to put them off. Her friends were amazing, but tenacious when they got something between their teeth.

And if she knew them at all—and she did—they weren't going to let this go. Better to get the hoopla over with so she could go back to brooding, because she was honest enough with herself to call it like it was.

However, when she opened the door, there was no mistaking that the person behind the diner bag stained with grease was definitely male. She couldn't see his face around the bag, but didn't need to.

Tatum's hand tightened around the edge of the door. Let him in or tell him to leave?

His other hand lifted a telltale box tied with a red gingham ribbon.

"I come bearing gifts."

"You fight dirty."

He leaned sideways, those green-gold eyes of his peeking around the box, mischief and humor swimming through them.

His expression was so different from the horror, anger and desperation she'd seen him struggling with last night that it simply took her breath away.

This was the boy she'd fallen in love with, impish and teasing, skating just along the edge of annoying.

He smiled. "Dinner, wine and dessert. I'm sorry for losing my temper earlier. Can I come in? Can we just share a meal, relax, maybe talk about a few things while emotions aren't running quite so high?"

She blew a heavy breath through her lips, fluttering her bangs. Her eyes greedily devoured the box he shook in temptation. It had been a while since she'd indulged in a treat from Sugar and Spice…she'd had a bridesmaid dress to fit into.

"Fine." Holding the door open, she let him in.

He didn't pause, but headed straight for her kitchen. She hadn't gotten around to showing it to him last night, but apparently he'd noted where it was anyway.

Not bothering to ask, he hunted for plates, silverware and wineglasses. She let him, watching the fluid way his body moved as he puttered around her personal space.

He'd always been lean and strong, covered in muscles that were a treat to the senses. But now she sensed a…harder edge to the body she'd once known as intimately as her own.

Even with his back to her and most of the room, he still managed to carry an air of vigilant, constant awareness, which left her exhausted just watching.

Evan dished out two burgers dripping with mayo, ketchup and mustard, piled high with lettuce and tomato. His had onion, but hers didn't. He remembered she didn't like it. That small gesture shouldn't have mattered, but somehow it did.

Taking out a giant container of fries, he divvied them out, unevenly because he gave himself at least double her portion. It was automatic. Something mundane he'd done numerous times during their relationship.

And so was her response. Walking across the room, Tatum paused long enough to steal one from his plate and pop it into her mouth.

"Hey, eat your own," he rumbled, false warning filling his voice.

She flashed him a taunting look and snagged another. "Not as much fun, handsome," she teased.

For a moment, it felt like this could be any night they'd spent together. Comfortable, familiar.

That is, until his body went utterly still, the easy camaraderie that had settled over them disappearing just as quickly as it had surfaced.

He swallowed. Tatum watched his corded throat work. After several seconds, he said, "Take as many as you want, beautiful," in a husky voice that sent an unwanted ripple tripping across her skin.

God, she'd always loved it when he called her beautiful. What woman didn't want to be reminded she was desirable to her husband?

Shit, this wasn't good. Fifteen minutes and she was responding to him like Pavlov's dog.

Breaking the spell, he turned away, popped the cork on the wine and poured them each a glass. It wasn't anything fancy, most likely from the market, but she gulped a huge swallow anyway, barely bothering to taste.

He pulled one of the chairs out from the table and held it for her, waiting silently until she sat.

Her body was stiff. She could feel him, heat and presence and just…Evan standing behind her. Did she want him to touch her or did she want him to pull away? Her brain screamed at her for one but her body begged for the other.

Slowly, his fingers brushed against her shoulder. Her eyelids slipped shut. Holy hell that felt good. How could such a simple touch fill her with the kind of bone-deep longing that ached?

Finally finding a small kernel of self-preservation, Tatum jerked forward, away from the caress. *Because* it felt so good. Because she desperately wanted more.

Taking the hint, he crossed to his own chair and sat. They both dug in, the silence settling over them far from companionable or soothing. There had been a time they could sit for hours without saying a word, because they hadn't needed to.

Now there was so much still left unsaid that the words filled the air between them, heavy and suffocating.

Pushing his plate away, Evan reached behind him for the wine bottle he'd set on the counter and topped off both of their glasses. He sprawled back in his chair, spreading out and taking up half of her little eating nook.

"We didn't have a chance to finish our conversation," he said.

"No, we didn't."

5

"Is there anything specific you want to know?"

He asked the question and then prayed she'd want information he could give her. Something that wouldn't make her realize just how close to the edge of "monster" he'd skated while undercover.

Something that wouldn't cause horror and revulsion to crawl across her expression the same way it crept across his skin.

Anything that wouldn't cement in her head that she needed to throw him out of her life for good.

He'd expected her to wonder how he'd spent the last three years, so when she asked, "How did your friends die?" he wasn't prepared. If he had been, maybe he could have held back the rush of memories. The chaos. The darkness. The startled screams and coppery scent of blood.

"They were shot." He could hear the dead sound in his voice, but couldn't stop it. That was the only way to deal. To shut down, shut them all out.

"You saw?"

No, he didn't want to relive anymore. "I can't, Tatum. You know there are things I can't tell you."

Reaching across the table, she snagged his hand. He hadn't realized he'd balled it into a fist until she slowly, gently, unwrapped each of his fingers so she could nestle her palm against his.

He stared at their hands for several moments, hers small and pale. Almost delicate, although that was the last word he'd ever use to describe Tatum. Soft. Her skin was so soft. Always had been. He could remember watching her sit on the side of the bed every night as she rubbed lotion into her arms, feet and legs.

He remembered the scent. Wanted it filling his lungs again. Needed it.

Surging up from his chair, he didn't register it scraping across the tile. He rounded the table and crouched beside her so he could cradle the warmth of her hand against his face, smell her scent.

And there it was, overlaid with the lingering note of the flowers she'd touched earlier in the day, a smell he'd always and forever label as hers. Sweet with a hint of musk. Clean.

That was what he needed right now.

Turning his head, Evan buried his lips against the center of her palm. He didn't kiss her or use the moment to seduce, neither of them wanted that. It was more, a flash of something deep. Despite having just gorged on food, his stomach suddenly felt cavernously empty. A hole only Tatum had ever been able to fill opened up inside him. Or maybe it had been there for a long time and he was just now able to admit the need because she was finally beside him.

Her hand trembled against his skin, and he knew she felt it, too.

But even as he acknowledged what was between

them, he could already feel Tatum pulling back. She wiggled her fingers, silently asking him to let her go.

But he couldn't.

"Can't or won't, Evan?" she finally whispered, her voice cracking on the words.

Shaking his head, he rose and reluctantly let her go. She'd seen straight through him, had always been able to do that. And not just with him. She was a superior judge of character with a top-notch bullshit detector built into her psyche.

"Maybe some of both," he admitted, sitting again. "There are things I don't want to tell you, Tatum. Things I don't want to think about. Stuff I've done I don't ever want you to know."

"Were you trying to do your job and keep yourself alive?"

"Yes."

"Then it wouldn't matter, Evan."

"You say that now, but…"

No sane woman would look at him the same if he spilled his guts.

"Look, Tatum, I know it isn't going to be as simple as picking up where we left off. I'm not stupid. But you're my wife. I'm on leave for several weeks. I want to spend them with you, try to figure out where we are, what we feel."

Whatever ground he'd gained with the gesture of dinner was immediately lost. He could see it in the way her expression simply shut down. Her shoulders curved and her arms came up to wrap around her ribs, almost as if she were protecting herself from an expected blow.

"You're going back?"

"Why wouldn't I? It's my job. It's all I know, and I'm good at it."

Her dark green eyes studied him, roaming across his face in a way that made dread drip steadily into his bloodstream. It looked as if she was memorizing him so she could say goodbye.

He wasn't willing to accept that.

"We owe each other a chance, Tatum. That's all I'm asking for."

"I don't owe you anything, Evan. You lost that privilege three years ago when you let me keep thinking you were dead."

"Then yourself. You owe it to yourself."

She scoffed, the harsh sound scraping through her throat. "What I owe myself is the promise no man will hurt me the way you did."

Damn, the pain shimmering in her emerald eyes nearly brought him to his knees. He'd done that. Although unintentionally, it hardly mattered.

Hell, he hated himself a little for doing that to her. He couldn't begin to think what she felt.

He definitely had his work cut out for him, but he wasn't a stranger to battling for what he wanted. And what he and Tatum shared was worth any sacrifice.

But the first step was getting his foot in the door.

Reaching across the table, he swept his fingertips along the edge of her jaw. He felt more than saw her sharp inhalation of breath and ruthlessly went in for the kill, stroking a tumbling lock of hair behind her ear and letting his fingers linger on the sensitive spot that always drove her insane when he sucked and licked.

"Let me stay, Tatum," he murmured in a low voice.

He trailed the slope of her throat, grazing the curve of her collarbone. Her skin pebbled wherever he touched. God, he wanted to kiss her. To replace the caress with the heat of his mouth.

She watched him, her eyes bright and wide. Her tongue snuck out to trail along her bottom lip. He wanted to lean in and snag it with his teeth, tug gently until she surrendered and let him in.

But they were balanced on a dangerous precipice and pushing now would give her an excuse to bolt in the opposite direction.

"For now," she finally breathed, the words wobbling just a little.

Round one, Evan.

Here was hoping he could pull out the ultimate win.

EVAN HAD BROUGHT DINNER. He was currently in her kitchen doing the dishes. And she was in the living room fuming.

He'd manipulated her. She knew it. Hell, she'd known it when he was doing it. And yet she hadn't been strong enough to stop him. A few well-placed brushes of his fingers over her skin, a plea dripping in that rumbling, bedroom voice that had always shot straight to her libido, and she'd folded like a bad poker hand.

Shit, she was in serious trouble.

Especially since, by his own admission, he had no intention of leaving behind the job that had taken him from her in the first place.

She hated to be the kind of ranting, crazy woman who demanded her husband give up a dangerous job because she couldn't handle the pressure. Actually, she refused to be that woman.

But she didn't think she could do it again and maintain any semblance of sanity. It would be much worse this time. She'd lived through losing him and knew how devastating it would be.

And there was no question in her mind. Through some miracle, the job hadn't killed him, but it eventually would. Luck ran out, and all things considered, Evan must be running on fumes in that department.

He hadn't shared the details of what happened, but between the nightmare last night and the hunted, faraway expression in his eyes when he'd briefly brought it up, she could read between the lines.

Water shut off in the kitchen, the light flipped off and then he was framed in the doorway, practically taking up the whole damn thing. Tucked beneath his arm was the box from Sugar and Spice. She'd completely forgotten about it until that moment.

In each hand he held their refilled wineglasses. Because that was what she needed, more alcohol and a fuzzy brain. The worst thing she could do was lose her inhibitions. She needed her wits and the constant reminders of why opening herself up to him again was a bad idea.

Evan crossed the space, soft yellow lamplight spilling over his body as he prowled closer. Tatum swallowed, trying to force down the lump of lust threatening to strangle her. Her body hummed, a constant pressure that made her restless.

Taking the glass, she didn't bother sipping before setting it down onto the table in front of her.

Evan folded his tall frame into the opposite corner of her couch. It was comfortable, the perfect place to settle in for a night of watching TV. Or it always had been, before tonight.

Now she couldn't shake this awareness, of him and her own body. Every pressure point beneath her skin throbbed. She should have taken the armchair, but if she got up and moved now he'd know how much he was affecting her. And that was knowledge she couldn't give him, because he wouldn't hesitate to exploit it.

The quiet shush of the ribbon as he pulled the chocolate box open shot straight into her brain, somehow amplified, and rubbed uncomfortably against her senses. He popped the lid and held the chocolates out to her.

She'd intended to refuse, but a quick glance inside stalled the words halfway up her throat.

Lexi's signature aphrodisiac chocolates were distinctive and easily recognizable. Tatum had never tried any. Why would she? She hadn't had a lover to experiment with. But she'd heard they were delicious.

Did Evan know what he was handing her?

Tatum's gaze bounced up to his. He stared at her, steady and unwavering, over the edge of the box. Dammit, she couldn't tell. He was too good at giving nothing away.

"I'm told they're excellent."

He snagged one of the truffles covered in a fine dusting of cocoa. He bit into it, the quick flash of white teeth reminding her just how much she loved it when he took nipping love bites of her skin.

Shit, she didn't even need to eat any of them for her body to rev.

His eyelids grew heavy, slowly lowering over a tawny, taunting gaze that sent shivers down her spine and had her fighting the urge to run screaming from the room in restless need and self-preservation.

"Mmm." The rolling sound rumbled up from deep in his chest. She could feel the echo of it tickling across her skin. "Different, but yummy. Cinnamon and honey. Try."

Holding out the other half of the chocolate, he waved it back and forth in front of her. She could smell the cinnamon and something else a little spicy. Chilies? She'd have to ask Lexi.

Tatum shook her head, trying to refuse. Evan scooted closer, practically touching the chocolate to her lips.

"What are you afraid of, Tatum?"

"Nothing." Irritation flashed through her. "I'm not in the mood for chocolate. Especially Lexi's aphrodisiacs."

He wasn't surprised, so he obviously knew exactly what he was trying to feed her. Which only made her irritation skyrocket.

With a shrug, he pulled back and popped the rest of the chocolate into his mouth.

Staring at the box, his fingers waving over the top as if he were playing eenie, meenie, minie, mo, he said, "You don't really believe that a little chocolate can make you do something you don't want to do, do you?"

"No." The single word came out hard and clipped.

His lips twisted into a knowing smirk. She wanted to wipe it off his face.

"So, does that mean you already want me and you're afraid the truffles will push you over the edge?"

Tatum hissed long and low. She'd walked into that one.

"No." Yes. That was exactly what she was afraid of. Several of Lexi's customers swore by her truffles. She had a booming internet business. Tatum dealt with enough customers to realize people wouldn't keep coming back for more if they didn't do something— even if it was merely a placebo effect.

Her body was already throbbing enough, though, and there was no reason to tempt fate and play fast and loose with her steaming urges.

Evan popped another one into his mouth and chewed slowly. Tatum watched the thick column of his throat work and fought the need to close the space between them and lick.

"So far," he said. "I don't get it. These things aren't making me any more aroused than I was the moment I walked in your front door." Lifting his penetrating gaze to hers, she watched, spellbound as he slipped his index finger into his mouth and sucked. He did it again, thoroughly cleaning chocolate off of each finger until she was practically panting.

"But then, I don't see how anything could make me want you more than I already do. Do you know how many nights over the last three years I've woken up, sweating and hard, with the echo of your cries ringing through my head? Or how many times I stroked myself, eyes closed, praying for you to be the one touching me?"

She couldn't breathe. The room spun, the only thing keeping her centered his glittering eyes full of heat and promise. The need was so sharp she could feel the cut of it deep inside.

Why was she denying them both what she desperately wanted?

She couldn't remember anymore.

To hell with it.

Tatum's body coiled, on the edge of launching herself at him, when he surged up from the couch and out of her reach. Dropping the open box of chocolates onto the table, he peered down at her.

"I didn't get much sleep last night so I'm heading to bed."

She watched him walk away, all fluid power. Tight jeans hugged his ass and thighs.

What the...? Well, hell.

The haze cleared, like fog slowly lifting to reveal a perfect spring morning.

He'd done that on purpose. Spun her up only to let her crash back alone.

Tatum huffed out an unhappy breath.

Two could play at that game.

HE COULD HAVE PUSHED, but he wanted Tatum to come to the decision that being together was right, not because her hormones were buzzing, but because she wanted him back in her life.

The tortured expression on her face as he'd walked away had just been a bonus. Although, that euphoria of triumph had been short-lived when he quickly realized Tatum wasn't the only one going to bed frustrated and unfulfilled tonight.

A high price to pay for scoring a point in round two, but worth it.

Collapsing onto the bed, Evan didn't bother pulling back the covers. He clasped his hands behind his head and stared up at the beige ceiling. His entire body throbbed. He could practically count the thump of his pulse lodged painfully against his fly.

Closing his eyes, Evan drew in a deep breath and tried to will his body to relax. One muscle group at a time, he forced the tension away. It was working, right up until a noise sounded in the room next door.

The thump was innocent, except for the vision of Tatum getting undressed for bed flickering against his closed eyelids. She'd never been the kind of woman who particularly fussed over her wardrobe. She'd dressed in sharp suits, skirts and blouses when she worked in an office. Obviously, she didn't need business clothes in order to run a florist's shop. He assumed her standard uniform had become the jeans and long-sleeved T she'd been wearing earlier.

That thought naturally led him to wonder if anything else about her wardrobe had changed. While the rest of her clothes had run toward the conservative, her underwear and nighties had always been the stuff of male fantasy—soft silks and satins edged with lace that flirted with the tops of her thighs and molded to her skin. Bright, bold colors—red, black, blue and green. No pinks or pastels for Tatum. It had always driven him insane when she'd walked out the door in the morning, knowing what she wore beneath the respectable layers of clothing.

And that he was the only one who'd ever get to see.

Now he could envision her slipping something sinful and sexy over her head and letting it skim down her body.

He was completely lost in the fantasy, which was probably why it took several minutes for the other sounds to filter through. A soft moan. Another thump. A whimper of need. And a telltale buzz that had a red fog filling his head.

Oh, no, she wasn't.

Especially not while he was on the other side of her damn wall, aching so badly the teeth of his zipper were probably permanently tattooed onto his dick.

Leaping out of bed, Evan tore the door to his room open. Without stopping to knock, he barreled into hers, eyes zeroing on the bed where he expected to find her.

But she wasn't there.

The room was dark, golden light from the attached bathroom spilling into the space. It took him a few seconds to find her, back pressed against the wall adjoining his room. Her arms were crossed over her chest, one elbow bent, her arm held up with a vibrator clenched tightly in her fist as it buzzed uselessly in the air.

The damn thing was purple. For some reason, the color pissed him off.

Her mouth was open and another moan slipped through, although it was obviously a lie. She glared at him, her green eyes hard and stark with emotion.

"Would serve you right if you'd walked in on me taking care of myself."

"Honey, we both know in that situation you wouldn't be taking care of yourself for long."

Tatum flicked the switch and the buzzing stopped, although the echo of it still relentlessly pulsed through Evan's brain. She tossed it onto the dresser beside her.

She'd obviously chosen her spot to maximize his torture, but she'd made one tactical error. Wedged between her dresser and the corner of the room, she had nowhere to go when he stalked forward and closed the distance between them.

He didn't stop until his body was flush with hers. He enjoyed her sharp intake of breath and the way her eyes widened. The way her body tensed and then melted against him. God, she felt so good.

"That wasn't nice," he breathed against her mouth right before he fused his lips to hers.

This time he didn't wait for her to open for him, but

took what he wanted, not that she resisted. Her tongue met his, stroke for stroke. Her fingers buried in his hair, tugging just a little and making his scalp tingle.

After several moments, she used that hold to pull him back. "Neither was what you did," she murmured, brushing her lips softly, seductively against his mouth. He could have broken her hold, but he was enjoying her teasing.

"If it's any consolation, I pretty much screwed myself with that stunt. Probably more than you."

"I don't know about that."

"You didn't eat any of the chocolates."

Her mouth curved, and he could feel her smile as she continued to drive him crazy. "True."

Evan grasped her hips, pulling her into the cradle of his body. There was no doubt she could feel just how much he wanted her.

Satin slipped beneath his palms, sliding seductively against her skin. Tatum moaned, and this time he had no doubt the sound was real. Her eyes darkened and her lips parted.

At least he had one question answered. She still preferred sexy lingerie.

Dropping his mouth to her throat, Evan licked at the pulse speeding there.

His fingers grasped the material at her hip and slowly began to gather it into a tight ball.

He wanted to see her. Explore every inch of her. Discover any changes to the body he'd known so well. But he'd settle for whatever she let him have. For now.

It didn't take long to bare the tiny scrap of matching lace covering her mound. And even less time to swipe it out of his way. His fingers brushed up the slit of her sex and straight into the slippery evidence that she wanted him just as much as he wanted her.

"It looks like we're both in a bad way."

She hummed, the sound full of dreamy surrender.

"Let me make you feel good, Tatum," he whispered against her skin. "Please, baby, let me touch you. Let me feel you. Let me replace all of the fantasies that kept me going with something real."

Her head dropped back against the wall with a muffled thump. She stared up at him with glassy eyes, and for a brief moment, he felt the tight pinch of guilt. But it didn't last. Not when she slowly nodded.

He was afraid to take the time to undress her. Reality was a looming giant, just waiting in the wings to come crashing in and reclaim the few minutes he'd stolen.

Caressing her thigh, Evan urged her to wrap her leg high on his hip. The scent of her arousal enveloped him, making him dizzy with need.

Bending down, he sucked the tight button of her breast into his mouth. The satin of her gown was slick against his tongue. She whimpered and arched up into the suction. He grazed his teeth over the pearled flesh, reveling in her choked sounds of pleasure.

Showing the same attention to the other breast, Evan reached blindly to the dresser. He searched, letting out a sound of triumph when his hand closed around the velvety surface of the vibrator.

With a thumb, he flicked it on, the gentle buzzing filling the room. Tatum jolted in surprise, her eyes widening as she stared up at him. Her heavy breath sawed through parted lips. His own chest ached with the pressure of wanting her. Needing her.

Slowly, he brought the purple tip to the inside of her

thigh and let it play across her skin. Evan held her in place, one demanding hand cupping the back of her head, refusing to let her look away from him.

The connection he'd always felt with her snapped between them, vibrant and intense.

He trailed the humming instrument up to the sensitive crease of her hip. His fingertips followed the same path, delighting in feeling the prickles raised on her skin.

She pulled in a sharp breath and her eyelids fluttered, trying to close.

"No," he whispered, "Look at me. Let me see." He wanted to watch her dissolve beneath the pleasure he could give her.

Her eyes sprang open, dark and deep. Such a vibrant green, like the dense rainforest he'd become so familiar with. No one liked the moist heat, but though his trips into the suffocating vegetation had been few and far between, somehow he'd always felt safer there. Less on guard. Comfortable.

Just the way he felt diving straight into Tatum's gaze.

Her neck arched into his hold, his fingers tunneling through the soft haven of her hair to the heat of her skin. Even as he lost himself in the reality of holding her, he moved the vibrator relentlessly closer to that delicious center of hers.

He let it play across the seam of her sex, torturing her even as his own body rioted in response. She gasped and groaned, writhing against him and trying to get him to move where she needed him.

"Please," she pleaded, the single word dripping into his blood like the sweetest honey.

He wanted to draw this moment out as long as possible, but didn't have the patience or strength to follow through.

Diving deep into the hot cleft of her sex, he found the straining bud of her clit and applied pressure. Her entire body bucked. Her thighs strained open wider, offering him more. She whimpered, but she didn't look away. She let him see absolutely everything she was feeling.

And he couldn't help but feel a thrilling moment of triumph. She wouldn't be able to keep him out, not after letting him see so much.

She was so close. He could feel her body winding tighter and tighter, the muscles right at the opening of her body fluttering with a need to be filled. He had every intention of giving her what she needed.

Evan dragged the vibrator down to rim her sex, teasing, before finally letting it slip inside her body. Bit by bit, he fed her the smooth purple surface. Part of him wanted to look down, watch her body swallow what he was giving her. But he couldn't pull his gaze from hers, he was so entranced by the intense pleasure suffusing her face.

He pumped the vibrating shaft in and out, his own hips involuntarily matching the steady, thrumming pace. She whimpered and whispered, "Oh, my…"

Her fingers dug into his back and shoulders, pinching and leaving marks. Her body undulated beneath him, shamelessly fighting for more.

And then she was crying out, the sound barely breaking free before his mouth dropped over hers so he could absorb the taste of her pleasure. She trembled, her entire body rolling with the force of her release.

God, she was gorgeous. On any given day Tatum was the most beautiful woman he'd ever seen. But when she was open like this to him…there was nothing greater. Her trust, need, innate sensuality, vulnerability and happiness all laid softly in the palm of his hand to protect and cherish.

Pressed tight against him, her entire body went lax. She clung, this time not with building tension but fluid relief.

And he felt like the strongest, luckiest, most invincible man in the whole damn world.

Right up until she pushed him away.

6

"WHAT THE HELL was that?" she roared, slapping at his chest and trying to shove him away.

The man was a veritable mountain. She knew the only reason he stumbled backward was because she'd surprised him. If he'd been braced...

He frowned. "That was me making you feel damn good."

They both knew she couldn't argue with that, not without looking like an idiot, and a lying one at that. She'd come so hard she was afraid he'd have scars on his shoulders from her nails.

Yanking at the hem of her nightie, she tried to find a shred of the modesty she'd obviously lost. It didn't help that her panties were utterly soaked as they settled back into place, snug against her still-throbbing sex.

"Don't play that horrified, affronted game with me, Tatum. What exactly did you expect to happen when you taunted me with this?"

He held up her purple vibrator, still glistening wet from her body. Heat, which had nothing to do with arousal, suffused her skin. Considering all they'd done and been to each other over the years, her embarrassment seemed out of place. But she couldn't stop the tide of bright pink as it swept up her chest and face.

She slapped back in the only way she could, with words. "I didn't expect you to charge in here and use it on me."

"Bullshit. That's exactly what you wanted. You wanted me to barge in here and overwhelm you so you could pretend you didn't have a choice, that you didn't really want me to touch and tease until your body was on fire."

Tatum opened her mouth to argue, but the words wouldn't come. Because, God, he was right. And up until he let her think he was dead for three years, they'd never lied to each other.

Evan had been the one person she'd opened herself up to. She'd let him see the worst of herself, which she'd hidden from the rest of the world—the guilt and grief and relief when her father had killed himself.

She was a terrible person, angry at her father for taking the easy way out, but at the same time feeling freed from the oppressive weight of being responsible for him and his pain. There had been days she'd resented having to live apart from her husband—a man she'd loved desperately. That she'd had to give up her dreams of college when her dad had lost his job and been emotionally unable to handle a new one when her mother had gotten sick. Resentful that, before she was ready, she'd had to become the responsible adult.

And then she'd hated herself for those feelings.

Evan was the only person she'd ever been completely honest with about her jumbled emotions after the devastation of walking in and finding her father lying in a pool of his own blood.

She couldn't lie to him tonight, not even if he'd earned it.

Seeming to sense her crumbling resolve, Evan closed the gap and pressed against her until she had no choice but to flatten against the wall. And immediately, her body responded to him.

How could he do that to her? Not five minutes after an amazing orgasm, she wanted more. Wanted *him*.

The long ridge of his erection nestled perfectly against the cradle of her thighs. He rubbed against her already sensitive clit, sliding silk over her slippery skin in a torturous caress.

"Don't do this, Tatum. Don't put walls between us that have never been there before. Give me two weeks. I can make you love me again." He leaned forward, brushing his mouth along the ridge of her cheek until he reached her ear. "I've never stopped loving you. You, Tatum, are the only person in this world who matters to me. I need you, now more than I ever have."

Her eyes slid shut. Hope and need and fear collided inside her chest, a heavy concoction that seemed to drag on every muscle.

"I…can't, Evan," she whispered, the words cracking because deep inside she didn't want to say them. But she had to. She needed to protect herself, because heaven knew no one else would.

No one had protected her against the pain of watching her mother slowly waste away from cancer. No one interceded when her father crumbled and she was left to try and hold both of their lives together, only to have him reward her sacrifice by taking his own life.

And no one stood beside her to blunt the pain of losing the only person who'd ever been there for her. Oh, there'd been people, but no one who understood.

No one she could talk to. Confide in. Even now, surrounded by friends she loved, and who obviously cared about her...she hadn't exactly opened up. Hell, she hadn't told them she'd been married.

Somehow she'd found the strength to keep going after she thought Evan died, but it had been touch and go. And she needed him to understand just how close to the edge she'd come.

"Do you know how tempting it was to follow my dad?"

Evan's entire body bucked, as if her words had been a physical blow.

He tried to pull away so he could look at her, but Tatum tightened her hold, keeping his face buried in the crook of her neck. She couldn't look at him and say these words. Hell, she'd barely been able to look at herself for weeks after the cowardly thoughts had invaded her brain.

"Those first days were bad, but there were people. Lots of people. Other wives. Your friends. Even your parents."

"Surprised they bothered to show up." His bitter words slipped across her skin. She didn't blame him for the response. His childhood hadn't been any better than hers.

His father was a mean drunk, his mother a weak woman who accepted the occasional slap and shove as nothing but normal. She hadn't tried to stop her husband from turning his beer-soaked anger on their only son. She'd viewed it as a personal reprieve.

Tatum hated to burst Evan's bubble at the thought his parents might have shown a modicum of parental feelings at his death. But his tone of voice said he probably wasn't harboring such thoughts anyway. "They showed up hoping they'd get some money. When I told them I was your sole beneficiary and had no intention of giving them a damn thing, they hightailed it back to Detroit."

"Where they belong."

Tatum hummed in agreement.

"But then everyone went away. People returned to their lives, as they should have, and I was left alone with nothing and no one."

A charged silence filled the room, until his voice, softened by regret and something more whispered against her skin, "You're not alone now."

No, no she wasn't. "No. I've found a place where I belong. Friends who matter and would do anything for me. And I'd do anything for them. Even the men in their lives have become important to me."

This time when he applied pressure on her hold, trying to dive back, she let him go.

His fingers slipped softly across her skin, down her throat, from the raised edge of one collarbone to the other.

"I meant me, Tatum. You have me."

"No, I don't, Evan. You said so yourself, you're going back to that life. And unlike before, I'm no longer willing to follow you."

MORE THAN TWELVE hours later, her words continued to echo through his head like the death knell of every dream that had kept him alive.

No, he wasn't accepting it. Despite the cool reserve she was trying to hide behind, she still cared for him. Definitely responded to him.

He wasn't the kind of man who walked away from a challenge, even when it might be the smart thing to do. He had a couple of weeks to make her change her mind. To show her they could have the life they'd lived before.

She was just scared. And, frankly, he didn't blame her.

However, her reaction only solidified his resolve to keep the full details of his time in Colombia from her. They'd bolster the defenses she was building. He didn't want those images floating through her head.

He needed a strategy.

Obviously, coming at her physically was on the agenda. He wasn't above using their sexual chemistry against her. But he needed more. Wanted to show her he could become a part of the life she'd built in Sweetheart—that he had no intention of taking that from her.

Somewhere in the middle of the night, he'd decided the best way to do that was to make himself useful around Petals. Not only would it show her that resolve, but it would double the amount of time he could spend with her...and crowd into her personal space.

Knowing he needed to be proactive about implementing his strategy, Evan was up early. He wandered out of the guest bedroom fully dressed and ready for the day to find her puttering around the kitchen, bleary-eyed and wrapped in a silky robe that did nothing to cover her body.

"Morning," he murmured, leaning against the doorframe and enjoying the view as she stretched up on tiptoe to reach for a cup on the top shelf of the cabinet.

She let out a startled squeak, spinning and sending the coffee cup tumbling to the floor. Without even thinking, Evan shot forward and snatched it out of the air. Crouched in front of her, he enjoyed the perfect view of a creamy thigh. The spicy, sweet scent of her invaded his lungs, spreading through him with a burst of heat. Immediately, he was rock hard.

Not good. At least, not right now.

"You scared me," she grumbled, her morning voice rough and full of accusation. Grabbing the cup from his hand, she turned back to the fancy coffeemaker on the counter.

Evan rose slowly, enjoying the view just as much on the way up as he had at the bottom.

"Sorry." Although he really wasn't.

Keeping her back to him and her focus on the machine, she said, "You're up awfully early. Big plans for the day?"

"That depends."

She popped a pod of coffee into the machine and waited as it whirred and bubbled. "On what?"

"You."

She finally shot him a look over her shoulder. Leaning opposite her, hands braced against the counter, he didn't miss the way her gaze swept down his body, lingering for a moment on his chest, abs and thighs.

Heat crawled up her skin. Evan fought the urge to smile in triumph.

Yanking her gaze away, she asked, "What do you mean?"

"Well, I figured the least I could do was come into Petals with you and help out. Give you another set of hands."

Before he'd finished the sentence, she was already shaking her head. "I don't need another set of hands. Especially ones that don't know what the hell they're doing."

"I'm a quick study, Tatum. Good for heavy lifting and getting...sweaty." He dropped his voice, letting a touch of innuendo and promise leak into his words, and watched as her shoulders stiffened in reaction.

He could see another protest coming, but cut it off. "I want to know what you do, Tatum. You know me. Either put me to work or spend the entire day with me loitering around the place."

"The sheriff's a good friend of mine."

"I'm sure he is."

"I can have you thrown out."

"You could, but you won't."

He pressed his body full-length against her back. Bending, he buried his face in the crook of her neck and breathed deeply, her scent now overpowered by the sharp tang of coffee.

"Back away, Evan," she said, no doubt her breathy words far from how she'd wanted them to sound.

He didn't touch her, not really. His hands settled against the counter, bracketing her hips. He could reach out and run his thumbs along her silk-covered skin, but he didn't. Instead, he let the idea of the caress torment them both.

"We both know you won't throw me out, Tatum. You aren't willing to make a fuss. No doubt the rumors about us are already flying through town. You won't want to add to them by making a scene in the middle of Main Street. And, rest assured, I'd be more than happy to make a scene."

"I don't like you very much," she seethed.

"Mmm," he said, just shy of the sensitive spot on the back of her neck that drove her crazy. "Probably not, but I bet your body's still slick and hot, begging you to forget everything and take what you want."

"When did you become an arrogant prick?"

Backing away, Evan let out a humorless laugh. "I've

always been an arrogant prick, sweetheart. That's one of the things you love about me."

Her cup slammed onto the counter, spilling dark brown liquid in a spreading stain as she finally whirled to face him.

Her palms shoved at his chest. "Back off, Evan. Now."

"I can't, Tatum." Brushing gentle fingers across her temple, he tangled them in her wild, messy morning hair. It was so soft, sliding like the finest silk through his fingers. "I won't."

With a disgusted sigh, she jerked her head away from him, taking the waterfall of hair out of his reach. "If I let you tag along, you have to promise to keep your hands to yourself."

"That's no fun."

"Maybe not, but this is my job, Evan. My livelihood. Petals is important to me and I won't let anything disrupt that, including you."

Inclining his head, Evan said, "Understood. What's important to you is important to me."

Blowing out a harsh breath, she said, "I really wish you wouldn't say things like that."

"Why?"

"Because they remind me too much of the boy I fell in love with."

"I'm still that guy, Tatum."

She speared him with those dark emerald eyes, locking him into place and stealing his breath. A mixture of emotions swirled deep enough to suck him under and make his chest ache.

"No, you aren't. But I'm not that girl anymore, either, so…"

With a shrug, she snagged her coffee and walked out of the kitchen.

Evan simply watched her leave. He couldn't very well follow her, even if every instinct in his head was screaming at him to do it.

How could he feel as though he'd taken one step forward by gaining entrance to Petals and still managed to lose ground?

SHE KNEW IT was a bad idea, but short of making an ugly scene, Evan was right, she didn't have much choice but to let him in.

She wasn't worried about him getting underfoot or slowing her down. Tatum had plenty of experience working in high-pressure environments, the skills gained working for a Fortune 500 company smoothly transferring to owning a small business of her own.

It was more the spectacle he provided.

She'd already anticipated the "March of the Town" as people dropped by to see if she'd spill any juicy tidbits about her life, knowing she wasn't the type to gossip about others, let alone herself.

With a twisted smile and a few well-placed sarcastic comments, she could have handled the gossipers. What she couldn't control was Evan.

Who, while offering to run the counter, was perfectly placed to charm the entire damn town.

By midafternoon they had a steady stream of customers, half of them citizens who'd never purchased a damn thing from her before today. At least her bank account would be grateful for the influx of sales.

Though she wondered if the headache pounding relentlessly behind her temples was worth it.

"Evan Huntley, Tatum's husband."

The first time she'd heard him introduce himself to Mavis Reynolds, an overly enthusiastic and nosy seventy-three-year-old member of the Sweetheart Bridge Club, she'd nearly swallowed her tongue.

"Husband? I didn't think she was married."

She'd heard at least twenty versions of this same conversation. And had to admit to reluctant admiration for the way Evan deflected every single one of the questions tossed his way.

"We've been separated for several years due to my job. But I'm here now and we're trying to work everything out." Somehow, he managed to make it sound as if he was simultaneously wholly responsible for whatever they were "working out," and completely contrite and ready to grovel at her feet.

The bastard. By midmorning he had the blue-haired set eating out of his palm.

Unfortunately, his current conversation had taken an unexpected turn.

A woman Tatum knew mostly by sight as a lawyer in town made a sound that was difficult to interpret. She was dressed in a smart business suit and tasteful black heels. Her hair fell into a perfectly sleek bob that hit precisely at her chin.

"Well, that's a relief. And explains why she never dated. You know, there were rumors around town that she played for the other team."

The woman, Tatum thought her name was Samantha, gave her a twisted, apologetic smile. "Not that there's anything wrong with that."

No, of course not.

Evan flashed her a knowing smirk, which caused a bolt of irritation to lance through her. She was intimately familiar with that expression. It meant he was about to do or say something he knew would get him in trouble…and, yet, he was going to do whatever it was anyway.

So frustrating.

"Trust me, she's definitely into men. A damn siren in bed."

Samantha shrugged, not raising an eyebrow at the personal information Evan let hang in the air. *Her* personal information. Yep, she was going to kill him.

"If you say so. There are plenty of other rumors flying around town now."

Evan leaned forward across the counter separating them like he was settling in for a good secret. "Really? Like what?"

"Oh, that you guys had a green card marriage."

He laughed, the smoky, seductive sound scraping down her spine. "Nope, we're both Detroit born and bred."

"Well," Samantha reached into the designer purse slung over her shoulder. "Either way, should you need a good divorce attorney, give me a call."

Divorce attorney, her ass. The look Samantha gave Evan left little question that she wanted to do a hell of a lot more than file a petition with the court for him.

The bitch had just hit on her husband. In front of her. Obviously, there was a reason she hadn't gotten to know Samantha well in the last two years.

Tatum's hands trembled from an unexpected roll of anger and jealousy. She fought the urge to reach across the counter and shake some sense into the predatory woman. Tatum had never been the kind for physical violence, no matter the situation or provocation. Just one more reason letting Evan back into her life was a bad idea. She did not like her reaction to Samantha's flirting, but unfortunately she couldn't seem to curb it.

The attorney grabbed the bundle of red roses she'd purchased—how unoriginal—and walked out the door.

Tatum's teeth ground together at the tinkling bell that chimed on Samantha's exit. Her gaze stayed glued to the spot where the woman had disappeared, a red haze washing across everything.

No, she was not going to tear out onto the sidewalk after her.

A soft chuckle finally broke through the grip of her rage. Tatum looked up to find Evan standing in front of her, staring down at her.

His eyes, more green than brown today and perfectly matching the T-shirt pulled tight across his massive chest, twinkled at her.

"Breathe, Tatum. And for God's sake, unclench your teeth before you break one."

She did as he suggested, only realizing the relentless ache stampeding through her jaw when she finally let it go.

"Not funny," she said.

"A little funny," he countered. "And a lot encouraging."

The rhythmic pounding in her head increased. Shit.

"My reaction has nothing to do with you. She's a bitch, plain and simple. What kind of woman hits on a married man in front of his wife?"

"A divorce lawyer."

"Apparently."

"I don't care about her. She's unimportant."

Sure, to him she was unimportant. Tatum was still fighting the need to draw blood. Which only pissed her off more. She shouldn't be feeling so…territorial over Evan.

But she did. Her chest tightened at the thought of him touching Samantha, popping the buttons on that damn suit and burying himself between her thighs.

Evan scratched his head. "What really interests me is the statement she made."

"Oh, yeah? Which one? The one where she suggested I was a lesbian or slid her business card to you implying you needed a divorce attorney?"

"The one where she said you haven't dated anyone in town."

She reeled back, shocked at his words. "I told you I wasn't seeing anyone."

"Present tense. You never said anything about not dating anyone. There's a difference."

Tatum gawked at him for several seconds before slamming her mouth shut. She watched in fascination as pain, regret and hope all flitted across his face.

"I'd understand, you know," he said softly. "I wouldn't blame you if you'd been with someone else." His words were gentle, no doubt meant to soothe her. Instead, they ignited the anger that was still so close to the surface.

"You're damn right you wouldn't blame me."

He swallowed, his Adam's apple bobbing up and down with the motion. "I told myself I wasn't going to ask, that I didn't have the right. But…I think I need to know so I can stop imagining every man who comes through the door has had his hands on you and is just here as an excuse to get another taste."

"You've been…" Only a few men had come into the store today, probably the few customers who were really shopping for flowers and not gossip. But now that she thought about it, Evan had been much cooler with the men than the women.

And that was strange. He'd never lacked for charm, that was for sure. But he spent most of his time with men. Guy's guys who shot shit and crawled around in the dirt. Went to strip clubs and got drunk. He'd never had a problem relating to other men.

She could lie to him. Part of her was ashamed to even entertain the thought. How pathetic did it make her look to admit she'd spent the last three years in a physical deep freeze because no man could compare to *him*? Not to mention that admitting the truth would only increase his resolve…and ego.

But she couldn't do it. Something inside wouldn't let her lie about this.

"No, I haven't been with anyone."

She half expected him to gloat. Or let some quip fly.

Instead, he cupped her shoulders and pulled her hard against his body. His mouth found hers, possessive, reverent, plunging them both into the deep end. Her brain disengaged, shutting off and leaving only instinct and response.

She clung to him, sinking into the sensations only he'd ever been able to make her feel. After several moments, he pulled back, softening and shifting from sizzle to simmer. Although her brain couldn't quite catch up.

"Thank God," he murmured into her mouth.

The bell above the door rang again. Tatum knew it meant something. She needed to…but the thought wouldn't form.

"Don't let me interrupt," came a sweet voice she recognized.

7

EVAN WANTED TO howl at the interruption. He considered ignoring whoever had walked into Petals. But even as he tried to deepen the kiss, Tatum was already pulling away.

She disengaged their mouths, turning her head to take in the intruder. With persistent hands, she tried to push at his arms holding her, but that's where he drew the line. He wasn't ready to let her go.

Instead, he shifted his hold, quickly spinning her around so her back was pressed to his chest, his arm slung diagonally across her body from shoulder to hip.

She tossed an unhappy glare over her shoulder. Evan just grinned at her.

He heard a muffled snort from across the room. "I suppose that answers my question. I was wondering how the chocolates went over."

For the first time, he bothered to take in the woman behind the interruption, Tatum's friend Lexi.

Her shop was about half a block away so he had to assume it was nothing unusual for her to stop by—or for Tatum to return the favor.

He didn't have to see Tatum's expression to know

she was frowning in response to Lexi's comment. Tatum's body stiffened against him and she shifted. Instinct kicked in and Evan flexed his arm, subtly trying to hold on to her. He wouldn't let her go. Not when it felt as if he'd finally gained a little ground. Not when, for some strange reason, it suddenly felt that if he stepped away from her, he'd be leaving a jagged piece of himself behind.

He couldn't afford to lose anything else. Tatum couldn't miss the ripple of his body against hers. Her sharp intake of breath shot straight through him. Along with the residual heat of their kiss, it was enough for the ridge of his sex, nestled against the small of her back, to harden.

There was no way she couldn't feel his response to her. While he hadn't planned it, she immediately stilled, abandoning her efforts to put distance between them.

He wasn't too proud to take a victory, however it presented itself.

Pretending he and Tatum weren't in the middle of a silent, physical conversation, Evan answered Lexi. "They were delicious. I was expecting to taste the herbs, but I really couldn't."

The blonde smiled, her grin lighting up the room. "What about you, Tatum?"

"Oh, I didn't have any."

Evan flexed his hold, letting his thumb slip beneath the hem of her shirt to tease the space right above her waistband. He could practically feel the electric hum shooting through her body.

Tatum slapped a hand down over his, pinning him and halting his teasing. Her grip was far from playful, taking his hand and squeezing until the bones practically rubbed against each other.

The comfortable smile he'd been sporting turned into a reluctant grimace. His girl always had been able to take care of herself. He admired that strength, always had, always would.

Using his discomfort as a distraction, she spun out of his hold. Snagging her other hand, Evan stopped her trajectory, leaned down and whispered so only she could hear, "That was sexy as hell," before letting her go.

Raking Tatum with a heated look, Evan tossed out an excuse to Lexi, "I'm going to head into the back and…do something."

TATUM WATCHED HIM LEAVE, fuming, embarrassed and turned on.

"Ooh, girl, that man is scorching."

"More like scorched earth. He won't take no for an answer."

Lexi cocked a single eyebrow. "Sweetie, that did not look like no."

"Well, then you read it wrong."

"I don't think so. You're all flushed. And fidgety. You never fidget."

Tatum realized Lexi was right. Her fingers were playing mindlessly with the small cards she kept in a stand by the register, stacking, counting, straightening. They'd already been perfect.

Snatching her fingers away, she flattened them against her chest and blew out a frustrated breath.

God, he was driving her batshit crazy.

Grasping her by the elbow, Lexi dragged her to the front door. She paused long enough to flip the sign from Open to Closed, engage the lock and then pulled her out onto the frozen sidewalk.

"Wait," Tatum protested. But trying to stop Lexi

when she was on a tear was like planting a pebble on a train track and expecting it to derail the engine.

Why did everyone in her life think they could just... move her where they wanted?

Frustration and irritation gave her the strength to dig her heels in and stop Lexi's forward momentum.

"Stop. Just stop," she shouted.

Startled, Lexi halted. At least she'd finally gotten her attention.

"What is going on? Where are we going? I have a business to run and can't just...leave, Lexi."

Her friend blew out a harsh breath, concern lurking deep in her eyes. "Yes, you can. The girls are waiting at Willow's with lunch. You're going to take an hour away from the parade of Sweetheart busybodies who've been hounding you all morning and we're going to make sure you're really, truly okay."

Tears stung the back of her eyes. She wasn't a crier, never had been, but knowing her friends—the women who'd come to mean so much to her in a frighteningly short amount of time—were looking out for her, even if she didn't think she needed them to, crumbled her defenses.

"Okay," she croaked, trying to swallow the lump in her throat.

Wrapping an arm around her shoulders, Lexi bumped a hip against hers and then hustled her around to the back of Willow's bridal dress shop. She didn't just run the place with her business partner, Macey, she also designed several of the dresses, which were famous around the world. But today the rooms she used to house her creations and nurture her talent had been cleared of satins, silks, beads and lace.

Three beautiful faces looked up at her—Willow,

Jenna and Macey. Spread out across a table was an array of sandwiches, salads and sweets from Sugar and Spice. A fine bone china set wouldn't have been out of place, but the girls had obviously decided the situation called for something much stronger than tea.

Wineglasses waited, filled with pale pink, bubbling liquid. Heavenly. Tatum's mouth watered and her stomach rumbled. All she'd had today was a single cup of coffee.

Evan was obviously screwing with her system in more ways than one.

The growling broke through the charged silence of her friends. Their laughter followed, washing over her like the warmest, calming tropical breeze. Dropping into a chair, Tatum simply let her body relax. It was the first time she'd been totally at ease since she'd seen Evan lounging against his bike.

Without saying a word, Willow picked up one of the glasses and handed it to her. Tatum took a huge sip, letting the wine flood her mouth and taste buds.

God, she needed this. Needed them.

As if they'd all been waiting for some cue, the chattering started. Lexi told a story about one of the guys working with Brett at the resort. Apparently, he'd tripped and fallen into a batch of quick-set concrete. Luckily, he'd gone in ass first so all they'd had to do was peel his hardening clothes off his back. But the guys had been so worried about getting him cleaned up that they'd left the concrete and it had hardened… with a perfect imprint of his butt.

There'd been talk of having it framed and hung in the employee break room when the resort was finished.

Macey picked up the momentum, sharing the latest bridezilla horror story.

Willow lamented her inability to come up with a Christmas gift for Dev. She'd accidentally—okay, purposely—gone snooping, found a gorgeous diamond necklace he'd bought for her and was now afraid the top-of-the-line wood chipper she'd already ordered just wouldn't do. Even if the man had been coveting it for the last two months.

The conversation made Tatum nostalgic for the little presents Evan used to leave for her because he knew this time of year was difficult. She didn't need diamonds, never had. Not when he'd shown her he cared with things like a can of silly string or a beautiful silk scarf he'd caught her eyeing. The women ate. They laughed. Tatum downed two glasses of wine, enough for her insides to feel warm and just this side of mushy.

They were picking through dipped strawberries, pieces of caramel apple, brownies, tangy lemon bars and cookies covered in a thick, gooey fudge when every eye turned to look at her.

Suddenly, the cookie she'd just taken a bite of felt like sawdust in her mouth, even if it didn't taste like it.

Tatum set it back onto her plate, taking another sip of wine to force the mess down.

Well, the reprieve couldn't have lasted forever.

"So," Willow said, drawing the single word out to several syllables in only the way her soft southern drawl could. "You want to tell us what's going on?"

"What's there to tell?" she asked, shrugging. "I thought Evan had been killed on a Special Ops mission three years ago."

No, that wasn't quite right. It went deeper than *thinking*.

"They came to me. At my office." Which was one

of the reasons she'd never been able to go back to work. "To tell me he was dead. I asked them how. Begged for details. Needed to *know*. Did he suffer? Was it quick? All they could say was he'd been on a deep cover assignment with several other members of his team, all of them gone."

Beside her, Willow sucked in a harsh breath. Lexi made a strangled sound and Macey covered her mouth with both hands.

Tatum just kept going. "I buried him, or what I let everyone think was him. They'd told me, because of the nature of the op, his body hadn't been recovered. That should have been my first clue."

Macey dropped her hands, the bridge of her nose beetling in righteous indignation. "How could you have known they were lying to you?"

Tatum shook her head. "According to Evan, they weren't. At least, not then. They really thought all the men had been killed. It was almost two months before he could get word to them that he was alive."

"Why the hell didn't they tell you then?"

"Because Evan told them not to."

Jenna let out a low, rumbling growl, and a brief smile flitted across Tatum's lips.

"By then his cover was so deep...he was afraid each day would make the lie real. He didn't want to give me hope only to have to lose him all over again."

"That's..." Lexi's voice trailed off to nothing.

Tatum looked around the table, taking in each face, all with varying degrees of the emotions she'd been fighting. Shock, disbelief, anger, grief...hope.

"Kinda sweet," Willow finally finished.

"Wrong, but totally sweet," Macey agreed.

"So, what are you going to do now?"

Tatum admitted the truth—to them and to herself. "I have no idea. I've been in love with Evan Huntley since I was seventeen. Losing him was the worst experience of my life."

"So getting him back should be the best."

"You'd think," she whispered so softly the other women had to lean closer to hear. "But I don't know that I could survive losing him again. I've built a life without him. One that I like. I'm content. Letting him back in would be setting myself up for heartache. What he does is dangerous. A miracle saved him this time. It won't be there next time."

"Content," Lexi said slowly. She exchanged a knowing glance with Willow. "You know that isn't enough, Tatum. Especially when the chance for more is standing right in front of you, steaming up your store so much the windows fogged."

"They did not."

"I sure felt the heat."

Tatum scoffed, the sound vibrating through her throat. "Sex has never been a problem for Evan and me."

"So…does that imply there were problems before all this?"

Her eyes widened. Slowly, Tatum shook her head. "No. Never. I mean, sure we fought, but always over stupid shit. You know, the stuff that just gets under your skin and rubs you raw until you have to let the irritation out. Evan was the person standing next to me when I dealt with my mom's illness and the horror of my dad's suicide. He's always been right beside me, telling me I could do anything I wanted to. Supporting me. Loving me."

She looked up from the center of the table, where

her gaze had been trained, to find four sets of wide eyes staring at her.

"And you want to give that up without at least seeing?"

"No, but I think I have to. For my sanity. He's… holding things back. I mean, there were always aspects of his work he couldn't share with me, but this is more. Goes deeper. The first night he stayed over, he had a nightmare. No, it was more than that. I found him crouched in the corner of the room like some hunted animal. He pinned me to the floor."

Lexi's hand dropped down over hers, tightening. "You're okay?"

"Yeah, I'm fine. He was…devastated when he came to. Pissed at himself. Worried about me. He drove away and I didn't see him again for hours."

"He needs help, honey. That's all."

Obviously, he needed help. Not that she was surprised. Anyone living through what he had the last three years would. And deep down, Tatum knew she hadn't even heard the half of what he'd experienced.

"He's keeping things from me. I feel like I don't know him anymore. Or, at least, there are pieces of him I don't know."

"Give it time, Tatum. He just got back from three hellish years. It's going to take more than a few days to deal with that. To open up." Willow said, her voice soft and soothing.

Lexi nodded. "But in the meantime, it isn't going to help if you're holding back, too."

Tatum shook her head, those damn unwanted tears stinging her eyes again. "I don't know if I can do it. If I can open myself up again."

Willow ran a soft, soothing hand down her arm.

"You don't have to make that decision right now. You have to give him time, but you also have to give yourself time. Time to feel safe and comfortable with him again."

That was part of the problem. She did feel safe. And comfortable. More than she really wanted.

"Today, all you have to do is head back to Petals, open up for the afternoon and take things one minute, one hour at a time."

She knew Willow's words were meant as a comfort, but something about them weighed heavily on her chest. It was difficult to pull in a full breath.

Until Lexi sent her a knowing grin full of mischief, "And if I were you, I know what I'd be doing with the first hour, making those windows steam again. Your husband is smokin' hot."

Willow leaned forward, shoving Lexi sideways. "Not helpful, Lex."

"That's what you think. You didn't see the two of them together. Or the way our solid, practical and aloof Tatum melted into a puddle at his feet."

"I did not."

Lexi patted her arm, giving her a sympathetic look. "Oh, you did, honey. You totally did. But don't feel bad. Brett has the same effect on me. When he's around, I swear I can't think of anything else."

"That's just hormones."

Lexi shrugged, this time sending her a look of pure skepticism. "If you say so."

THIRTY MINUTES LATER, as she fumbled with the front lock at Petals, the only thought running through her buzzing brain was Lexi's suggestion to steam up the windows.

She couldn't get the damn key into the lock. It kept moving. The lock, not the key. Bending closer, Tatum squinted, filling her slightly blurry field of vision with the troublesome lock, and braced a hand on the frame, hoping that would solve the problem.

A metallic scraping sound made her glance down at the key clutched in her fist. It wasn't even in the lock yet, so how had she opened it?

Before she could puzzle that out, the door swung open. She stumbled, flailing for something to grab onto.

If Evan hadn't caught her, she would have ended up on her ass in the middle of the cold sidewalk.

He tugged her inside. In some small part of her brain, Tatum heard the click of the lock being engaged again. Hmm, not good, although she couldn't remember why.

"You walked out, without a word, to get drunk?" he asked, wrapping a hand around her arm and propelling her through the storefront and into the back workroom.

"No. I'm not drunk," she protested.

His snort of disbelief seriously rubbed her the wrong way.

"I'm pleasantly buzzed. Give me twenty minutes and I'll be stone-cold sober."

"Wonderful," he gritted out between clenched teeth.

Evan maneuvered her into a chair. Tatum let her body slump into the welcoming comfort. Her limbs were deliciously loose.

Slowly, her gaze traveled from the tip of Evan's scuffed motorcycle boots, over worn jeans hugging tight thighs, up the plane of his flat stomach and wide chest to a set of shoulders that could carry the weight of just about anything.

God, he was perfect. He'd always had a hell of a body, but whatever else Colombia had done, it had taken his strength and honed it into a work of art.

She was simply drinking in the view, her body reacting to him and burning with a fire that had nothing to do with the alcohol she'd drunk with lunch. Right up until her gaze collided with his glaring, sparking, pissed off eyes.

"I had no idea where you were, Tatum."

"I'm a big girl, Evan. I've been taking care of myself for a long time."

"Yes, you have, but that doesn't mean I don't worry."

She let out a harsh laugh. "Welcome to my world, then. How do you think I felt every time you went off on another top secret assignment?"

Some of the heat leeched out of his expression, softening him in a way that was far too tempting for her own good.

"You never said anything."

"No, I wouldn't, would I?"

Slowly, Evan folded his body until he was crouched in front of her. His fingers slipped across her skin, up her arms and into her hair. "No, you wouldn't," he whispered. "I walked back into the front room and you were just…gone." His voice went husky, not with heat but fear. "It was my worst nightmare, Tatum. The thought that kept me up every night I was in Colombia. The men I was dealing with there were ruthless. Perfectly capable of tracking you down and making you pay for my sins if they discovered who I really was."

She could see the genuine fear crawling through

him. The bone-deep agony of not being able to do anything about it. Of not being able to protect her.

Leaning forward, Tatum slid her fingers across his skin. His cheeks were covered with stubble, the scrape of it making her fingertips tingle. Running the pad of her thumb across his bottom lip, she enjoyed the way air gushed past as he exhaled a deep breath.

His hand clamped over hers, stilling her exploration. He held her tight, motionless against him, not pulling her hand away, but not letting her continue.

"I don't know that I can take much more, Tatum. Not without losing what little control I have left. Three years is a really long time and I ache, sweetheart."

For her. He ached for her. She heard the need soaking his words. Felt the echo of it deep inside her own soul.

She flexed her fingers, testing the strength of his hold and then realized it didn't matter. Her other hand picked up where he'd stopped her, trailing softly down the front of his shirt to settle over the bulge behind his fly.

His eyes screwed shut, in pleasure and pain.

"You're drunk."

"Not enough that I don't know exactly what I'm doing, Evan. Besides, isn't there something about this that's perfect? I was a little drunk the first time you made love to me."

"Yeah, but so was I. And I'm old enough now to realize that wasn't smart—or honorable."

She squeezed, stroking her hand up and down until he let out an involuntary sound of satisfaction.

"I don't remember asking you to be honorable. What I want is for you to touch me."

8

GOD, HE WANTED TO, more than anything. Any good intentions he'd had evaporated beneath the heavy weight of Tatum's hot, needy gaze.

He'd never claimed to be a good guy, anyway.

Grabbing her hips, Evan lifted her into the air. Her hands slammed onto his shoulders, digging in. He loved the way she clung to him, instinctively pressing her body against his for balance.

Slowly, he lowered her again, letting gravity and friction drive him crazy as he settled her onto the worktable that earlier had been spread with flowers, stems and leaves. Now it was blessedly clean. In his fantasies, she'd come to him late at night, surrounded by shadows and moonlight. They'd spent the entire night entwined together in a soft bed.

But that wasn't available and he wasn't giving her a chance to change her mind, not now that she'd finally decided to let him back in. There'd be plenty of time later to rediscover each nuance of her body.

Now, he simply needed to feel connected to her.

Tatum leaned back on the worn wooden surface, her elbows taking all of her weight. She looked up at him from beneath those long, inky lashes, her eyes glittering with the same rushing heat storming through his body.

She didn't wait for him to make a move, not his Tatum. Once she made a decision, she jumped in with both feet. Reaching for the buttons on the long-sleeved plaid shirt she'd thrown on with her jeans this morning, she lazily popped each through its hole.

Part of him wanted to grasp the edges and tear the damn thing open. The rest of him was too entranced with the show.

Each inch of skin she painstakingly revealed made his mouth drier. He wanted to run his tongue down into the shadowed V between her breasts and inhale the sweet scent of her deep into his lungs.

Scalloped edges of black lace appeared, cupping firm breasts. He remembered the feel of her covered in silk filling his mouth. He wanted that again with nothing between them.

Finally, she reached the last button, and the two halves of her shirt fell completely open to pool onto the table beneath her.

God, she was gorgeous. "Perfect," he breathed, unable to tear his gaze away from the stretch of pale skin. She looked so soft. The absolute opposite of everything that had filled his world for so long.

And he couldn't keep his hands off her anymore.

Swooping down, he placed his mouth right in the center of her stomach, sucking, licking, nipping. The muscles beneath his lips rippled in response and her body arched. Reaching around her, Evan found the clasp holding the bra in place and unsnapped it, but the straps were caught beneath her shirt.

Pulling her up again, Evan cradled her against his

body and deliberately stripped the barriers away. All of them. In the fantasy he'd long ago abandoned, he might have taken the time to appreciate the matching lace panties that covered her sex, but he was too far gone for that, shoving them off her thighs to drop to the floor tangled together with her jeans.

Tatum let out a sharp hiss as her bare bottom connected with the cool surface of the table, but she didn't move away. Instead, she leaned back, letting her legs fall open to show him everything.

Her sex was pink and swollen. Wet. Just begging for his touch. And he wanted to give her that. Wanted it for himself, too.

Stepping back, Evan simply took in the sight of her, his gaze roaming across every delectable inch of his wife's body.

"God, Tatum, you destroy me."

She laughed, a low, sultry sound that shot straight to his groin. "I don't want to do that, Evan. Especially not before you touch me."

Arching up, she offered herself to him in a way that was both erotic and humbling.

"If you don't stop staring and start doing, Evan, I'm going to start without you." She settled a hand against her taut belly, and her fingers flexed, then slowly traveled up toward the tight peak crowning her breast.

His entire body trembled, coiled with conflicting desires—let her follow through on the threat or touch her himself?

Maybe later he'd watch her play. Evan stepped between her spread thighs and leaned over her prostrate body. He sucked a nipple hard into the hot recesses of his mouth.

She moaned, the wicked sound ricocheting through

him. Her fingers buried deep into his hair, holding tight. Tugging, Evan let his teeth scrape across her skin, gliding over the taut pearl of her nipple with just the hint of pain before laving away the sensation with his tongue and replacing it with the warmth of spreading pleasure.

Tatum writhed, her hips arching in silent demand.

"Soon," he whispered against her skin as he trailed kisses up her shoulder and neck, and across her collarbones. "Soon, baby, I promise," he soothed.

Her fingers scrabbled across his body, searching for a way into his skin. He could feel them, unsteady, as she fought against the buttons holding his own shirt together. He let her fight, enjoying the time it gave him to tease and explore.

To reacquaint himself with her body.

Evan noted each time his touch stalled her movements and sent her breath stuttering. The crease of her neck and shoulder. The pulse pounding behind her ear. The bottom ridge of her ribs. The pad of his thumb barely brushing over the reddened tip of her breast.

But eventually, she completed her task, sweeping the shirt from his body to join the rest of the clothes on the floor. She didn't pause before tackling his fly, tearing at the button and yanking against his zipper.

Self-preservation had him taking a step back and finishing the job for her.

The blaze of those bright green eyes devouring him was like the fiery caress of a match struck against his skin. He'd never given a shit what anyone thought of him. But it mattered that Tatum liked what she saw.

With a single crooked finger, she commanded him to come closer. Sitting up, she watched him move and placed one hand low on his hip even as she urged him the last few inches.

The edge of the table bit into the tops of his thighs, but he didn't care. How could he while her hands ran across his body, down his chest to play over his abs?

Her mouth joined the party, landing softly on his left pec. Before she said anything, he knew what she would ask. "This is new. What does it mean?"

The hot point of her tongue laved his skin in a pattern he'd memorized. How many times had he let his fingers follow the same path, tracing the dark ink he'd added only a few months into his ordeal?

His hand cradled the nape of her neck, fingers buried in the silken waterfall of her dark hair. Evan closed his eyes and dropped his head, enjoying the thrill of her touch.

He'd wanted a reminder, a piece of her that only he could hold and know. Something to get him through the lonely nights and difficult days.

"Sekhmet, an Egyptian goddess. She's a warrior and protector." His voice trailed off to a whisper. "A healer."

When he'd first gotten it, he'd desperately needed a protector. To feel that he wasn't alone in the hell he was inhabiting. It was comforting to think of Tatum as a warrior goddess, a piece of her there battling beside him, urging him on and giving him something to fight for.

But now, now he needed her soft hands, warm lips and welcoming body to heal him.

"Is that the head of a lion?"

"Yep, the fiercest hunter."

"Her body is…seductive."

Evan smiled. He didn't have to look down to see the tattoo, he had the image memorized.

"Of course. She's you," he said, the words low and charged. "How I remembered you. Wanted you. A touchstone to keep me focused on why I had to stay alive. And come home to you."

She made a soft, choked sound, but didn't stop tracing the dark lines inked onto his body. He didn't realize she was crying until the warm splash of a tear hit his skin and rolled, leaving a wet trail.

Evan framed her face with his wide palms. The emerald eyes that had been filled with naked lust not five minutes ago were now awash with tears, which made his entire body cramp with regret and grief.

"Don't," he whispered right before bending to kiss the salty trail away. "Don't cry for me."

"I shouldn't be. I shed enough tears already. But…" Her arms tightened around his waist, pulling him closer as she shook away the rest of her thought. "Love me, Evan. Please. Now."

The frenzy that had overwhelmed them both was gone, replaced by something deeper and more profound.

Gripping his shoulders, Tatum used her hold on him to balance as she spread her thighs wide. He was perfectly poised, the swollen, throbbing head of his erection nudging against the slippery entrance to her sex.

She wrapped a hand around him, guiding him to where they both wanted him.

He was inside an inch when reality reared its ugly head. "Wait," he said through clenched teeth. It was taking everything he had not to simply thrust forward and bury himself deep inside her. "Condom."

Even before he'd finished the word, Tatum was

shaking her head. "Neither of us has been with anyone else and I have an IUD."

There was a small part of him disappointed to hear that. Before he'd left, they'd talked about her going off birth control when he returned. He wanted to give her that, to start a life deep inside her that they'd both love and share.

So, no matter what, he'd never leave her alone again.

But he was smart enough to realize that wasn't an intelligent impulse right now.

"You're sure?" he asked.

"Absolutely."

With a guttural groan of relief, Evan pushed home, burying himself in her welcoming flesh.

The heat of her engulfed him, blazing through and burning him from the inside out. He didn't care. He'd gladly go down in flames as long as he could do it wrapped tight in the clasp of her body.

She emitted a single sigh, the sound of it nearly bringing him to his knees. Relief, pleasure, comfort, tenderness.

Evan wrapped his arms around her body, simply holding her and relishing this moment. Finally being home.

He could feel the thrumming pulse of her sex. The way her muscles clenched and released greedily around him.

He slid his hands down the smooth surface of her back, relishing the tiny shudder she couldn't stop. Eventually, the pounding pressure to move swelled to the point of agony and he couldn't hold back anymore.

Hands planted wide around her hips, Evan tipped her body off center so he could control the angle of each stroke. Pulling back, he plunged deep again, rev-

eling in her sharp hiss, the way her eyes glazed over
with pleasure and her fingers dug deep into his skin,
dragging him closer.

Tatum's hips surged off the table. She arched into
his hold, trusting he would be there to catch her. And,
just like that, the frenzy returned, a bone-deep need
to touch every inch of her. To hear the cry of her release and know he could bring her to that mindless
burst of pleasure.

They moved together, perfectly choreographed after
years of experience and knowledge. He drove each
thrust right against that secret spot buried deep inside her. The need to let go burned at the base of his
spine, but he ignored it, focusing completely on her.

Incoherent noises of need tore from her throat.
Sweat dewed her skin, pale pink with the flush of her
rising release.

And then it was there, screaming out of her with the
sound of his name on her lips. Her body bucked, milk-
ing every last molecule of pleasure he could give her.

The tight fist of her sex, clamped hard around his
aching erection, was more than Evan could fight. His
own orgasm ripped through him, pulling an answering cry to tangle with the dying echo of hers.

His legs buckled. At least he had enough brain-
power to realize that the edge of the table probably
wasn't the best place to land. Pulling her with him,
he rolled them both to the floor.

It was cold against his overheated skin, but good.
Or maybe that was the euphoria of having Tatum
curled against his side.

He had no idea how long they lay tangled together.
Long enough for the sweat to dry on his skin. His fingers trailed in mindless patterns across her soft skin.

She shivered against his caress, but didn't move away, which was a good sign.

Part of him had feared that the moment they were both satisfied Tatum would try to pull away again.

"Mmm," she murmured, stretching against him. "There's nothing about this floor that's comfortable."

"Not true," he countered, placing a kiss on the crown of her head. "You're pretty damn comfortable."

She laughed, the pleasant sound rolling over him.

Could it be this easy? If he'd thought having sex would solve all their problems, Evan wouldn't have waited.

Planting her palms against his chest, Tatum shoved upward, gathering her feet beneath her. He thought about snatching her back down beside him, but realized, as much as he would have liked to, they couldn't stay huddled on her floor all afternoon.

Gathering their clothes, she tossed him his, his shirt smacking him in the face. By the time he disentangled himself, she was already half-dressed.

"Damn, you did that way too quickly."

Tossing him a saucy smile over her shoulder, she bent to tie the laces on her shoes. "Which just means you get to peel me out of them again later."

Hope and happiness swelled in his chest. "Promises, promises."

Evan watched her finger comb her tangled hair, sigh a battered sound of disgust and dig an elastic band out of the drawer in the nearby table so she could pull it up into a messy ponytail.

Evan moved a little more slowly, dividing his attention between her and his clothes.

Only Tatum had ever been able to make re-dressing somehow just as sexy as undressing.

The annoying ring of a phone interrupted his scattered thoughts. It rolled through their peace for several moments before he finally asked, "Are you going to get that?"

Tatum shook her head. "It's not mine."

Shit. He'd forgotten what the ringtone of his new cell sounded like. There were only a handful of people who had the number and none of them mattered because Tatum was standing in front of him.

But he wanted the interruption to stop. So, with every intention of silencing the damn thing, Evan reached deep into the pocket of the jeans still crumpled in his fist and fished out the high-tech gadget.

And then cursed when he saw the number on the display.

SHE'D GIVEN IN and they'd had sex. On her worktable.

And then she'd watched, bewildered, as Evan had hightailed it out of her store like his ass was on fire.

Without a backward glance.

While she'd still been struggling to right her clothes.

Tatum had no idea what to think of that. She definitely knew how to feel about it, though—pissed. And the fact the damn man had now been gone for six hours without a word was only cranking up her temper. And her insecurity.

Evan had always been a conscientious lover, even as a teenager. He carried an intensity that, when it was turned on her, was not just smoking hot, but reassuring. That laser focus had always made her feel wanted, desirable.

At the moment, doubts plagued her, crawling beneath her skin and making her restless.

It had taken everything to keep her concentration on Petals as the afternoon wore on. At first, she'd worried. There were few things that could have Evan jumping that quickly to disappear—and none of them good.

Around five, she'd broken down and texted him, simultaneously berating herself for the sign of weakness even as her thumbs tapped out the words. She'd never been the hovering wife and didn't like the idea of becoming one now.

But the worry had eaten at her.

Which did nothing to downshift her temper once it got rolling.

Without word from him, she'd gone back to her empty house—which, up until tonight, had always seemed perfect, but was now too damn quiet. Pulling a chicken breast out of the freezer, she'd decided to invest the time in making herself something yummy to eat. But the chicken stir-fry might as well have been glue in her mouth.

And at each sound outside her window, Tatum's body stiffened, in hope and then disappointment as it became clear none of them were the rumble of Evan's bike pulling into her drive.

God, she was being an idiot.

But she couldn't seem to stop. Her emotions were all over the map. She thought about pouring a glass of wine in an attempt to mellow out, but after what had happened this afternoon, her stomach churned at the thought.

She could call any one of her girls and they'd be over in a blink to offer her an ear, shoulder or distraction, whichever she needed most. The problem was, she wasn't sure and…she didn't want to admit to any of them she'd lost her head and let Evan have her in the back of her workroom.

So she simply sat, feet tucked up under her as she watched TV, although if anyone asked her what the shows were about, she wouldn't have been able to say.

Eventually, she gave up, locking all the doors, shutting off lights and heading to bed.

Unfortunately, that only increased the sensation of loneliness and disappointment that had been clawing up from her belly all night.

Screwing her eyes shut, Tatum tried to force her brain to shut off. It took a while, but eventually her exhausted body overrode her overactive mind and she drifted to sleep.

AND THAT'S HOW Evan found her several hours later. She looked so…peaceful. He almost hated to disturb her, but after the night he'd had, he needed to feel close to her. More than anything.

But he took the opportunity to unabashedly stare at her first.

She had an antique iron bed. The scrollwork above her head was gorgeous, with a patina that spoke of loving care and age. Most people, looking at her, wouldn't take Tatum for an antique kind of girl. But, maybe because her own history had been so rocky, she'd loved to find these kinds of treasures buried beneath dust and history. Forgotten, so that she could lovingly reveal the beauty that had been hidden.

With so much space, it didn't escape his notice that she wasn't sprawled out, taking up the entire bed. Instead, she was on *her* side. Where she'd always slept when they were together.

Her long, lithe body was curled in on itself, the

curve of her spine almost more than he could ignore. He wanted to run his fingers down her body, but just managed to stop himself.

She was hugging a pillow, her cheek resting on the fluffy mound, her hip cocked and her thigh thrown over the pillow in a way that made him want to take its place so her warmth would be draped across him.

What was she wearing beneath the covers? Another one of the confections that nearly made him swallow his tongue? Her legs were obviously bare, because moonlight glinted off the pale skin of the one she'd worked outside the blanket. It had always amused him that she would have the covers pulled up to her nose, but one foot out so she wouldn't get too hot.

Although, it didn't much matter what she was wearing, because it wouldn't be on for long.

Slowly stripping off his own clothes, Evan left them in a pile on her floor. Walking around to his side, he placed a knee on the bed and watched her body roll toward him with the dip. But she didn't wake up.

Slipping beneath the covers, he tugged until they fell out of her tight fist to pool at her waist. Tonight she was wearing a rose-colored nightie trimmed in elegant black lace. A mix of tradition and tease.

He trailed his fingers across her shoulders, tugging at the poor excuse for a strap. It easily slithered off her shoulder. He followed it, letting his hands play across her back, ribs and hips.

Scooting closer, his fingers brushed the low edge of her neckline, teasing, relishing the way her nipples pebbled into hard peaks. In her sleep, Tatum sighed, the sound full of need and relief punching straight through him.

Unable to resist, he slipped his hand beneath the

soft satin to cup her plump breast. With sure fingers, he plucked at her, dragging a harder, sharper sound from her throat.

She was so warm and languid pressed against him. He wanted to take her soft and easy. To bend her knee and spread her wide, slipping into her from behind and just rocking them both to delicious oblivion.

But the moment her brain engaged, Tatum had other ideas.

"What the hell are you doing?" she cried, rolling out from under him. Before he realized what was happening, she was out of bed, standing in a pool of moonlight with both arms crossed protectively over her chest.

From the glare she was giving him, it was clear they were going to have to deal with something before he could coax her back into bed.

So much for hoping the wild frenzy they'd shared this afternoon would be enough to break through whatever was holding her back.

With a sigh, Evan pushed upright, planting his back against the cold metal of the headboard. Crossing his ankles, he settled the covers around his waist so they could both concentrate on whatever was coming and get it over with so he could get back to making love to his wife.

"Are you…" Her deep green eyes went saucer wide. "Are you naked?"

"Why wouldn't I be?"

"Because this is my freaking bed, Evan. Because I didn't invite you into it."

Her incredulity might have been humorous if the heat behind her words wasn't burning so clearly through her gaze.

"Oh, but you did, sweetheart. This afternoon."

"Letting you screw me in my workroom hardly constitutes an open invitation into my body and bed."

Okay, now *he* was pissed off. No longer worrying about keeping anything covered, he shoved up from the bed. She took two steps away—smart girl—but he caught her. He didn't slow her motion, not until her shoulders and hips settled against the solid barrier of wall.

Hadn't they been here once already?

For each step forward he thought he'd gained, Evan somehow kept looking up to find himself three steps backward instead.

Leaning close, he pressed into her personal space. "Let's get one thing straight, angel. What happened this afternoon was me making love to my wife after three long years apart. Sure as hell was intense, but it was far from screwing."

Trailing his fingers down the expanse of her throat, thrilling just a little when she had to swallow against the tangle of emotions his caress caused, he watched her reaction. The way her pupils dilated, her skin flushed. Her breathing became ragged. Her fingers curled into the wall, as if she was trying to find a steadying hold.

He could have told her the only thing she needed to cling to was him.

After several seconds, she finally whispered, "You left me."

And the hurt that climbed up to swamp her gaze nearly brought him to his knees.

9

TATUM WATCHED THE hard edge that had cut across his features soften. His body followed, the tension slowly leaking out.

The backs of his fingers brushed across her skin, from collarbone to collarbone, sending a ripple of tingles rocketing through her.

"God, Tatum, I'm sorry. I didn't think…" His words dwindled off to nothing, but she heard what went unsaid. He hadn't considered how she would feel or react.

Tatum had no idea what to do with that. It definitely didn't make her feel good. In fact, it made her spine crawl with restless uncertainty.

She waited for him to say more, but his mouth stayed stubbornly shut.

When she realized he wasn't going to offer anything else up, she couldn't stop herself from asking, "What happened? Where did you go?"

His jaw tightened, grinding his teeth together so tightly she feared a few might break.

He was going to tell her it was classified. She could see it in his eyes. If he did, she would tell him to leave.

And that would be the end of their marriage.

Pain ripped through Tatum's chest, so strong and quick she nearly doubled over with the unexpected hit of it. But Evan's strong body prevented her from giving in.

She was so preoccupied with her own spinning thoughts it took several moments before she realized he was speaking.

"I got a call. From…a contact. About the cartel in Colombia. There's movement. Unexpected movement."

It was almost as if the words, once said, had released a flood of information that had been dammed up behind them.

"The takedown was tightly coordinated, crushing the top twenty or thirty members of the group. They were spread across the country, some in Bogotá, some in Barranquilla, some peppered through several smaller communities and a few hidden deep in the jungle."

Evan's gaze dragged up, catching a spot on the wall inches above her head. Tatum realized he wasn't seeing her bedroom, but another life she had nothing to do with. Even his voice had changed, taking on the faint hint of an accent, the melodic tones of the language he'd instinctively been speaking that first night in his sleep.

It was as if a part of him had slipped back into the person he'd been when he was gone.

"In the melee," he continued, "we were able to keep my cover intact by letting the joint task force take me down, as well. For anyone who wants to look, there's a paper trail leading back to my cover's extradition to the U.S. on bogus drug charges I had fled from. The thought was that the few low-level thugs left to pick up the pieces would have too much on their plates to worry about tracking me down."

A frown pulled his dark brows into a deep V over

his ever-changing eyes. They were a pale green shot through with threads of golden brown.

Why was she focusing on that and not the meaning behind his words? Maybe because it was easier. And less frightening.

"Apparently, we were wrong. Someone's been following up. Asking questions."

"Are you in danger?"

Evan finally looked at her, not that it did her much good. He'd always been stellar at hiding behind a mask whenever he needed to. And something told her his three years away had only helped him hone those skills.

"No." The single word was hard and left no wiggle room for doubt.

And yet…

"Why don't I believe you?" she whispered, her stomach churning sickly.

He brought his hands up to her face and cupped her jaw. His thumbs brushed softly, hypnotically, down the slope of her throat, even as he dipped close enough to stare into her eyes.

"I promise, Tatum, I'd die before I let anything happen to you. You're safe."

That she believed. Unfortunately, it didn't make her feel better. It made her feel worse.

"That isn't what I asked, Evan."

He didn't respond, at least, not with words. Instead, he claimed her lips.

She should struggle. Stop him. But she couldn't.

Not when her entire body was overwhelmed with how good his kiss felt—soft, gentle. She could practically taste the banked heat and passion he was trying to hold back.

Her resolve wavered. Her head screamed at her to

push him away. Her heart thudded desperately inside her chest. And the rest of her body throbbed, all her nerve endings awake and alive in a way they hadn't been in so long.

As much as she knew she should, she couldn't do it.

Grasping his wrists, Tatum arched into his hands, silently communicating she wanted more. Wanted him right where he was. At least, for now.

The rest she'd deal with later.

Much later.

Groaning, Evan gathered her close. He picked her up, urging her thighs around his waist as he backed blindly away from the wall. He didn't look behind him. He didn't take his focus off of her.

A shiver of anticipation shot through her.

He was hot and hard against her, not just his erection, although that was certainly impressive. But all of him. His shoulders, arms, thighs. Solid beneath her as he held on.

For the first time since he'd walked back into her life, Tatum finally felt safe. The problem was that the sensation would be fleeting, and she knew it.

Eventually, he'd have to let her go.

Putting his arm beneath her rear, Evan boosted her higher, into position so the length of his sex nestled perfectly against her. She was damp. So wet that he slid against the satin-covered well of her sex as smoothly as if there'd been no barrier between them.

Each motion as he moved backward bumped the head of his cock against the swollen bud of her clit. It was divine torture and Tatum whimpered at the maddening sensation. Because it wasn't enough. She needed to feel him moving deep inside her. Claiming, filling, touching something only he'd ever reached.

But Evan had other ideas.

She expected him to hit the bed and roll, putting her beneath him and immediately slamming home.

Instead, he simply fell, letting her sprawl across his body. Before she had a chance to catch her breath, Evan's hands dragged her gown over her head.

The slide of satin against her skin had always made her feel feminine, beautiful, desirable. But it had nothing on the experience of his fingers running across her body.

The way he watched her, gauging her reactions with that piercing, haunted gaze…

Pushing up with her palms on his chest, Tatum tried to put some distance between them, to get some perspective and a grip on what was happening. But Evan was having none of that. He climbed up on his elbows, reclaiming the inches she'd taken, bringing their bodies flush again.

His mouth found the crook of her neck and sucked, hard. A trail of prickles chased across her skin and every nerve ending in her chest burst to life with a fiery, hot tingle.

Evan urged her up, and she resented the space he put between them…right up until she realized why. Without taking his mouth from her skin, he worked her panties down. Out of the way.

With a sigh of pleasure, she rolled her hips, sliding against the hard press of his erection. Evan hissed. His hands, hard at her waist, dug deeper.

"More," she breathed. "I want more."

The ache burning deep inside intensified, threatening to expand and engulf her like a supernova. And still she kept rocking against him, unable to stop herself from taking the pleasure of sliding him between the swollen lips of her sex, coating him with the evidence of her desire.

Gripping her hips, Evan urged her up onto her knees. His erection sprang free and immediately found her slick entrance.

Without waiting for him to tell her what he wanted, Tatum took what she desperately needed.

Slowly, she sank her body onto his, taking him in. Her thighs trembled with the force of holding back, but the feel of him was too good to rush.

"Angel," he uttered in a desperate groan, his fingers digging into her hips. He tried to get her to move, but Tatum wouldn't budge. She simply sat, relishing the feel of him lodged deep inside. The stretch and burn. The throbbing ache.

The sensation of…relief. Release. Not the sexual kind, not yet, but of her heart. Her soul. The thing that had been walled off and encased in ice since the day they had told her he was gone.

Grasping her wrists, Evan pulled them out from under her. She collapsed onto his chest, her sensitive nipples dragging against the hard planes of his body.

Entwining their fingers, Evan leaned up and crushed his mouth to hers. This kiss wasn't foreplay— it was connection, history, memories. It was the familiar taste and feel. It was being able to find him in the dark with nothing but sound, scent and sensation.

Bringing their joined hands back to his chest, he broke the kiss, pushing her slightly away. But it didn't matter, the connection stayed, an invisible rope binding them irrevocably together.

His eyes flashed green and golden, burning with the same fire of need that consumed her.

She could see every emotion rampaging within

him. He made no effort to hide them. Desperation, desire, lust, love. A blazing need that both scared and thrilled because it overwhelmed.

"Take what you need, Tatum. Let me give it to you," he whispered, his hips bucking so he could drive deeper. Her internal muscles spasmed, clamping hard around him, even as a whimper fell from her lips.

And, just like that, she couldn't stay still, not any longer.

Their fingers tangled, his unflinching gaze locked squarely on hers, she did exactly what he urged. She took. Riding him, letting her physical need overwhelm them both, a frenzied race to the peak of oblivion that was so close but just out of reach.

Because she wanted it with him. She didn't want to go over alone.

Her eyelids fluttered closed, but she snapped them open. His own dropped, but he didn't take the glitter of his longing from her, either.

"Please, Evan. I need you," she begged.

As if that was all he'd been waiting for, he moved with her. Meeting each of her downward strokes with a deep plunge of his own. They found a rhythm, their rhythm, and got lost inside the rough slide, damp skin and panting breaths.

Releasing her right hand, he flattened it against his chest, and held it. The racing beat of his heart thrummed against her palm.

Without thinking, Tatum took his other hand and placed it palm down against her own chest.

Something sharp flashed through his gaze, flaying straight to the bone and laying everything he kept hidden bare.

Panic surged, but it was no match for the orgasm

rocketing toward her. Too late to stop it, her body gave in, convulsing with the force of what he made her feel.

His name screamed through her parted lips. Her fingers clenched tight, holding on to the only solid thing left to her, *him*. The room swam out of focus and all she could see was Evan, his beautiful eyes, intense concentration and the ragged edges of his own release.

The hot flood of his orgasm filled her. His hips pistoned, driving through the tight clamp of her muscles, caught up in ecstasy. Her name was on his lips, too, but it wasn't a shout of relief. It was a whisper. An answered prayer, given with quiet reverence.

Absolutely spent, Tatum collapsed. Their legs tangled, sweat-slicked skin against sweat-slicked skin. Now, she couldn't just feel the slow gallop of his heart against her hand, but against her entire body. And the pulse of it rumbled just beneath her own skin. Vibrated with the aftershocks that fluttered through her sex, over and over and over again.

Sweeping her disheveled hair out of her eyes, his fingers gently played across the skin at her temple. His lips found the crown of her head. And he whispered, "Baby."

Tatum squeezed her eyes shut.

What had she just done?

FIVE DAYS LATER, Tatum's head still spun. Standing at her worktable, she stared into space.

The bell above the front door shot her out of the mental black hole she'd disappeared into. Shaking her head, she waited to hear the low rumble of Evan's voice as he greeted the customer. In the last couple of days, they'd fallen into a pattern, and she still wasn't sure if it was comfortable or uneasy. It just was.

They spent their nights burning up the sheets. In those hours together, Tatum felt more connected to Evan than she ever had before. But in the bright light of morning, all the concerns and fears drifted right back in. She was on a mental seesaw, unsure how long she could hold out and endure the ride.

At Petals, she'd been handling all the back-office stuff. Arranging flowers, ordering from wholesalers, fulfilling phone and internet orders. Evan looked after the retail space. He was charming, and everyone who walked through the door seemed to genuinely like him. Not a surprise; beneath the tattoos and intense eyes, he was a great guy.

She'd taken to pausing, whenever a customer came in, to listen as he helped little old women choose flowers or advised some guy in the doghouse how to get out. He knew more about flowers and their meanings than she ever would have guessed.

But that probably shouldn't have surprised her. During a slow period yesterday, she'd caught him researching online. When she'd asked why, he'd said Petals was important to her, so learning everything he could was important to him.

The comment had made her sigh. And sent a pool of fear flooding her belly.

She waited, but after several moments she still hadn't heard the rumble of his voice.

Eyebrows beetled in confusion, Tatum walked through the door separating the retail space from her workroom. She greeted the customer with a distracted smile, her gaze sweeping the small area for Evan.

It was pretty clear he wasn't there. A flash of something through the window caught her attention. She stepped forward, stopping a foot away from the huge plate-glass window.

The December chill seeped through the barrier, soaking into her skin. She spotted him on the sidewalk several stores down, surrounded by the shoppers rushing to quickly buy Christmas presents from the surrounding boutiques on their lunch hours.

Tatum hugged herself, running hands up and down her arms to settle the goose bumps that had erupted across her flesh. It was because of the cold, not the sight of Evan, a hard expression pinching his face as he growled into his cell phone.

It wasn't the first time she'd caught him moving away to talk on the phone. Or text. Or email. And each time he had, the severe expression on his face had become...harder.

Whenever she asked him about it he brushed her off. Or distracted her. But he never answered her questions.

And that did absolutely nothing to settle the ever-increasing jangle of nerves that seemed to fill her days.

"I'm sorry," a soft, gentle voice sounded at her elbow. "Could you help me? I want to send a poinsettia to my son and daughter-in-law."

Shaking her head, Tatum turned to give her customer a smile, but she knew it didn't really come off as genuine.

"Sure. Just follow me over here and we can fill out the delivery order. If you'd prefer, you're welcome to pick out whichever one you'd like to send." Tatum swept her hand across a modest display of the plants in several shades of red, pink and cream.

"That would be wonderful," the friendly woman said, veering over to choose one.

Twenty minutes later, after answering several questions about the different colors, their history and possible meaning, the woman finally made her selection, filled out the form and paid.

Normally, Tatum would have been more tolerant of her indecision. It was clear, because she mentioned it, that the daughter-in-law was new and the woman wanted to make sure her gesture was well received. They'd had a rocky start, apparently.

It was the kind of thing Tatum enjoyed, a moment when her work could possibly help resolve a situation or make someone's day brighter. These customers were much better than the cheating spouses who often came in to order flowers for both their wives and girlfriends.

But Tatum was impatient, and the longer the woman took, the more restless she became. Evan hadn't returned, and from her vantage point behind the register, she couldn't tell if he was still pacing the same spot on the sidewalk.

The minute the customer left, Tatum hotfooted it over to the window only to find him gone.

He'd left again. Without a word.

Anger bubbled inside her chest, slowly filling her up.

While she was spending her nights baring herself and practically spilling her guts at his feet, sharing her business and the life she'd built without him, he was keeping secrets. Disappearing without a word and expecting she'd just...accept it as she'd always done.

But things were different. She was different. And she wasn't going to do this.

She'd worked up a healthy head of steam when the front bell rang again. Hopping off of the stool she'd collapsed onto in her workroom while brooding, she didn't get two feet before Evan's voice greeted her.

"I ran over to the pub and grabbed us lunch."

Tatum stopped inside the doorway, staring at him. He smiled at her, his eyes filled with a glittering mischief she easily recognized. Dropping her gaze to the front door, she noticed the bolt had been turned, locking them into the store alone.

Evan held up a brown paper sack as though he'd been out hunting and gathering and bagged an antelope instead of walking a few blocks and ordering a couple of burgers.

Okay, so he hadn't disappeared the way he had the other night. Or, not exactly. He had still walked out of Petals without telling her. And taken what was obviously a rather contentious phone call.

Crossing her arms over her chest, Tatum forced her gaze from the bag up to his face.

"Who were you talking to earlier?"

The smile disappeared, and Tatum realized it hadn't been real. Oh, the glimmer of intent and desire had been, but the rest of it was a well-crafted act.

"Damn, you're probably so flipping good at your job," she said before thinking about the consequences of sharing her thoughts.

His mouth twisted into a frown. "What are you talking about?"

"If deep cover work ever dries up, you should really try Hollywood. They'd love the hard-edged, scarred, bad-boy vibe you've got going."

He raked a hand through his hair. "I have no idea what you're talking about."

"Yes, you do."

"Look, I'm sorry I walked out and left you with a customer."

"I can handle my customers just fine, Evan. I was doing it long before you showed up and I'll be just fine handling them when you're gone again."

God, she wanted to believe that, but the longer she spent with him the less she did.

He'd seamlessly inserted himself into her life. Before, the only thing that had gotten her through was that there were no memories in Sweetheart. She didn't see him every time she went to a movie, grabbed a drink with a friend or walked through her front door.

Now he'd be everywhere.

"What are you talking about?"

Shaking her head, Tatum decided it wasn't worth arguing over the inevitable. "Nothing. Just, the next time you need to pop out, give me a holler so I don't leave a customer standing up here for five minutes."

She spun away, letting the door to her workroom crash closed behind her.

But she didn't get far. Evan smashed through, grasping her elbow and turning her around to face him.

"Look, Tatum, I apologized. What more do you want from me?"

"Nothing, Evan. I don't want anything from you."

Only that was the biggest lie she'd ever told. She wanted everything from him, with him. But she wasn't going to get it. Better to face reality now than in a few weeks or months when he disappeared again. Or really got killed.

"Then why are you angry?"

"I'm not." Lie two. Or was it twenty?

He dragged her closer, bringing their bodies flush.

"You are," he whispered silkily. "I just can't figure out why."

"You're a smart man," she taunted, "I'm certain you'll work it out eventually."

God, she hoped not. The last thing she needed was for him to realize just how tied up in knots she was right now.

He stared at her for several charged seconds. His eyes, more brown than green, glistened with suppressed anger of his own.

Good.

"The phone call," he said.

Tatum jerked her elbow, her frustration—and temper—escalating as he kept a firm grip on her arm. "Give the man a prize."

His features softened. The pressing bands of his fingers eased. "It's nothing, Tatum."

"Bullshit, Evan. I know you, and that call was not nothing."

"Fair enough. It's nothing I can tell you about."

"Hmm." She somehow managed to fill the sound with every ounce of sarcasm she possessed. This time when she jerked away, Evan let her go.

His mouth worked, as if he were chewing on words. Were they words he wanted to say and couldn't, or words he knew he shouldn't voice because they'd just piss her off more? Did it matter? Either way, he stayed silent.

The sound of a hand banging relentlessly on her front door drifted back to them. They didn't move, though they could both hear the racket. Her door rattled with the force of each blow.

"Tatum," a voice hollered. "I know you're in there. Let me in."

_10_

SPENDING THE EVENING at the local pub was not how Evan had envisioned his night going. Not that he didn't appreciate getting to know Tatum's friends. They were important to her, so they were important to him.

Lexi's untimely interruption might have derailed a conversation he hadn't wanted to have, but it had also killed any chance he'd had to smooth things over with Tatum.

Hours later, she was still irritated. Oh, to anyone else she looked as if she was having a fabulous time. She might be able to hide the tension she carried from her friends, but not him.

He understood why she was putting on the front. Apparently, the bride and groom were back from their honeymoon and everyone had gathered at the local pub to share in the glow of their tans and stories about how beautiful their Caribbean resort had been.

Every man and woman present had managed to throw him a wary, calculating glance, cranking his already taut nerves tighter.

The phone call he'd received earlier had already set him on edge. A low-ranking member of the cartel who hadn't been rounded up with the others—because Evan had had barely any contact with the guy—had tripped an alert Evan's commanding officers had put in place.

The man had bounced around the country, entering the United States via the Mexican border. He'd taken a damn tour of the Southern states—Texas, Louisiana, Arkansas, Kentucky, Tennessee, Virginia, and finally showed up in Charleston.

Too damn close for comfort.

Every alarm bell he possessed had clanged when he heard the news.

Evan didn't believe in coincidences.

Lock had assured him they had things under control, were tailing the guy 24/7. Waiting for him to step out of line so they could arrest him and bring him in. Unfortunately, Evan hadn't gathered any evidence against him while in Colombia so they needed something new.

So far, the guy seemed to be lying low. So why couldn't Evan shake that itchy, uncomfortable sensation that told him he was being watched?

Tipping his beer bottle to his lips, he swallowed the last, warm dregs. He'd been nursing the thing all night, unwilling to indulge. He needed his instincts sharp, especially with Tatum close.

Looking up, he realized there was a good reason the hairs on the back of his neck were standing on end. He *was* being watched. Three sets of hard, male eyes were cataloguing his every move.

The women had naturally separated into a little group. They were sipping pink, fruity drinks. Well, everyone except Tatum. She'd never been the kind for fussy cocktails. She was a wine or whiskey girl. He'd always liked that about her.

The girls laughed and chatted, the rush of their conversation not registering in his brain. Something about a hammock and giant lizard.

What mattered to him was that each time he tried to touch Tatum she shifted away. She wouldn't meet his gaze, not really. She was unfailingly polite, sending him a couple of smiles that never quite connected. Distant. And that distance was slowly driving him mad.

If they'd been home, alone, he would have cut straight through it by kissing her senseless, but something told him making a scene in front of her friends was not the way to gain back the ground he'd obviously lost this afternoon.

But that meant he'd been basically left alone with three men he knew nothing about.

On the surface, he and Gage—apparently the groom—should have had something in common. Someone had quickly pointed out Gage had once been with the Rangers. At the introductions, they'd eyed each other over the lips of their bottles and given a chin nod. It wasn't as if they could swap war stories or compare scars. Everything they'd both done was probably classified at the highest level.

The other two men he'd met before, although he'd been a little too preoccupied to get their names. Brett and Dev belonged to Lexi and Willow.

They'd been sitting together at the small bar table for the better part of an hour, none of them making any effort at small talk. Not that he necessarily needed the welcoming committee, but...

The way they were watching him said the committee wasn't anywhere close to being called into duty tonight.

"You guys married when she was eighteen," one of them finally said, nodding over to where Tatum sat with her back to him.

Evan nodded. "Yeah, and I shipped off to basic a couple days later. Things were rough for her, mom sick and dad unemployed. It wasn't the greatest situation, but I wanted to take care of her the best I could."

Gage grunted, sent him a grudging look of respect before burying the look in his own beer bottle.

"I knew I'd marry her from the time I was about seventeen." Evan shrugged, the gesture full of the bone-deep acceptance he'd felt even then. "I've always loved her."

"Jesus, man. That's…" Brett glanced at the women, his voice trailing off.

A wicked smile twisted Dev's lips as his gaze landed on Willow. "I knew Willow when we weren't much older. Screwed it up, too. Big time. Wish I could get back the years we both missed."

Evan picked absently at the wrinkled label around his bottle. "God, I'd give anything to give the last three years back to Tatum." He couldn't stop his own eyes from finding her in the tight knot of friends at the high bar table several feet away. "But I can't do that."

The three men glanced at each other and then, in unison, settled back into their chairs. The tension that had filled their tiny table was just…gone. Like that.

"So, how'd you manage to fuck up?" Gage asked.

"Huh?"

"Tatum's obviously pissed, although she tries really hard not to show it," Gage said, signaling to their waitress across the bar to bring another round.

Evan shook his head, but then decided he probably shouldn't turn his nose up at the friendly gesture. He should have known an ex-Ranger would pick up on the tiny signs.

Evan's gut instinct was to pretend everything was fine, even if now it was obvious no one would believe the lie. He had a hard time sharing with Tatum, a woman he loved and had known for over half his life. These men were strangers.

But they were Tatum's friends and clearly cared enough about her to be wary and protective. If he was going to stick around and become a part of her life here...

"We had an argument about a phone call."

"Were you talking to another woman?"

"No, my CO."

Brett and Dev threw Gage a look that said, *help me understand, dude.* Gage simply shrugged.

"Why would that send her into a tailspin?"

"She's worried. Some things I thought had been handled have ended up being more complicated than expected."

"Is she in danger?"

He also should have anticipated that Gage would drill immediately down to the most important question. Evan flashed him a glance full of respect and understanding.

"No."

The other man frowned. "Are you?"

Evan hesitated. The people around him, people he trusted, were telling him no. But his instincts...they were screaming. But maybe that was just carryover from his time in Colombia. Maybe he was struggling more with settling back into the real world than he'd thought or anticipated.

"I don't think so."

Gage stared at him, hard, easily reading the meaning behind his hesitation.

"Man, if you need anything let me know. Tatum's one of us and we take care of our own."

Evan's pulse throbbed. "I can take care of my wife."

"Not saying you can't, just that if you need backup, it's here."

"Appreciate it, man." But he had no intention of taking the other man up on his offer.

Because nothing was going to happen to Tatum. He would not let the stain of his life touch her.

Everyone let the subject drop. Dev turned the conversation to college football and the domination of the Southeastern Conference. The conversation drifted over Evan's head and he turned his focus to Tatum.

Sometime while he'd been bonding with the other men in her life, his wife had gotten up and wandered to the bar.

Every seat was taken so she'd wedged herself between two men and was leaning across the worn wooden surface talking with the massive guy standing behind the bar. He managed to cock his head in her direction and listen even as he pulled several bottles from the well and mixed a couple of drinks.

Tatum tossed him a quick smile and then settled back on her heels when he walked away. Her head turned to take in the game filling the TV screen behind the bar. Her arms were folded, but her feet kept moving. She bounced up and down on the balls of her feet. The woman was constantly in motion, even when she stood still. Not that he minded. How could he when every bounce had her tight jeans hugging the delectable curve of her ass?

Desire scorched through him and settled painfully against the straining zipper of his fly. Damn, he wanted to take her home and burn that temper off between the sheets.

He was so caught up in the view of her straining thighs and round rear that it took him several moments to realize the guy sitting on her right had taken advantage of her proximity by wrapping his arm around her waist.

Evan shot up in his chair, feet planted on the floor ready to vault up and protect her.

But Tatum beat him to it.

Slamming her palm down over the guy's wandering hand, Tatum tossed him a blistering look and said something he couldn't hear.

"Who is that guy?" Evan asked without taking his gaze off her.

"Who?" Brett asked even as Gage was saying, "No clue, never seen the guy before."

That damn itchy, uncomfortable sensation crawled up the back of his neck. "That usual?"

"It isn't *unusual*."

"We are a tourist town," Dev said.

Brett shrugged. "But December isn't exactly the height of our season."

The guy in question didn't take Tatum's hint, snaking his hand out to touch her again the moment her attention turned back to the bartender.

Evan didn't wait for anything else to happen. In a few, ground-destroying strides, he was across the bar. The guy's fingers had barely brushed against her before he snatched the offending digits away.

Applying pressure, Evan twisted the guy's wrist. The man whimpered, his entire body shifting with the move in an attempt to relieve the painful squeeze.

"Keep your hands off my wife."

Tatum gasped, whipping around. Her green eyes catalogued the situation with lightning speed. He would have expected to see gratitude. Instead, they narrowed to tiny slits, and the glare wasn't directed at the grabby asshole.

"Let him go," she barked, glancing pointedly where he held the guy prisoner with little effort.

Growling, Evan did what she wanted, throwing the guy's arm away with disgust.

"You're married?" Mr. Grabby frowned, his words slurring as he looked accusingly at Tatum's left hand. "You aren't wearing a ring. How's a guy supposed to know if you don't wear your ring?"

Grabby sent Evan a pleading look, searching for male solidarity and understanding.

Evan wasn't in an understanding mood.

All around them conversation had stopped.

Crossing her arms over her chest, Tatum cocked out a single hip, the glare ramping higher. "I suppose, technically, I'm married."

"Technically," Evan ground out, his jaw aching with the effort to hold in the spew of words threatening to erupt. "Technically?"

"Technically," Tatum countered, her voice calm and cool.

Oh, he'd show her technically.

Without sparing a single thought to their audience, Evan swept her into his arms. Her eyes went round, realizing a few beats too late just what he intended.

Bending her backward, he bowed her over the bar and claimed her mouth.

And that was all she wrote. The kiss might have started because he was angry and frustrated. But the second he touched her, everything else evaporated.

As it always did with Tatum.

The pub could have exploded around them and he wouldn't have noticed, not once he had her soft sweetness opened for him.

Her hands slammed onto his shoulders. Evan had no doubt she'd meant to push him away. But she didn't. She had as much success controlling what they had together as he did—which was absolutely none.

Her fingers gripped him, hard enough that he thought he heard the seam of his shirt tear. Not that he cared. He'd buy a new shirt every damn day if he needed.

One of his palms settled between her shoulder blades, preventing the bar from biting into her flesh. The other sneaked down, cupping the ass she'd been tormenting him with not five minutes ago.

She whimpered and opened her mouth wider, inviting him deep inside.

He had no idea how far they would have both gone, except someone loudly clearing their throat cut through the sensual fog hazing his rationality.

Evan glanced behind Tatum to take in the bartender, a knowing smirk playing across his lips. Plunking several glasses onto the bar at Tatum's back, he said, "Five chocolate cake shots," and walked away.

Around them, the noise started up again, although it held a manic edge—voices overly animated and bright, conversations that weren't really about anything, so everyone could pretend they weren't paying attention, even though they totally were.

Evan grabbed the shot glasses and stepped back. Tatum's hands slid from his shoulders. Her eyes were glassy, as if she'd already downed all five shots.

Pulling in a deep breath, he watched her steady herself. Hated to see the desire melting from her expression.

Stepping out of her way, Evan let her pick a path back to the table. He dropped the shot glasses in front of each of the women who stared at him, wide-eyed and speechless.

"Enjoy, ladies," he purred before walking back to his own table.

They weren't far enough away to muffle the sound, and whichever one of her friends said it didn't really make an effort to try, but Evan couldn't stop the smile of satisfaction that tugged at his still-tingling lips when he heard, "Holy shit, girl, that was hot."

GOD, IT *WAS* HOT. Two hours later at home, her body still ached from the force of Evan's kiss. How could he so completely blindside her? After all these years?

Hell, her brain had shut down and she'd forgotten they were in the middle of the *pub* with half the damn town watching.

No doubt the Sweetheart telephone tree had already been activated to spread the news to anyone unlucky enough to miss the show in person.

Groaning, Tatum squashed her eyes closed and fought the rise of a blush. She wasn't normally the kind of woman to get embarrassed. She'd gotten over caring what other people thought of her a long time ago. She hadn't had the luxury of time to spend on stupid things like that. Not when her mother was dying and her dad was losing his mind.

Perspective could be a dangerous thing.

But here in Sweetheart...life had been easier. Calmer. She'd taken the time to get to know the people. And whether she liked to admit it or not, what they thought of her mattered.

And not just because she was a business owner in the town and a tarnished reputation could hurt her bottom line. They were her friends.

Flicking off the heels she'd been wearing since early morning, Tatum let out a soul-deep sigh of relief and tossed her purse onto the bench just inside the front door, not caring where it landed.

She collapsed onto the sofa, and relaxed into the soft cushions.

She loved going out with her friends, but it definitely drained her. And seeing how Hope had glowed and Gage had barely taken his eyes off his new wife... had made her happy. Not that they weren't sickeningly in love long before the wedding.

Evan entered the house, quiet and contained. He'd been that way all night. Actually, he'd been that way for days, and that was draining her, too. His constant alertness caused her own instincts to go haywire, like a magnet pulling a compass needle off point.

She closed her eyes, just listening, letting the sounds of him filter in. The quiet click as he closed her front door and twisted all the locks. The clink of her purse chain as he hung it on the hook nailed to the wall, which she never actually used. The soft tread of his footsteps across her floor.

She wanted to be upset with him, and maybe tomorrow she'd uncover the irritation that had set her on edge all afternoon. But right now, it had completely disappeared. Damn the man.

Her temper wasn't a match for Evan's kiss, which was not news to her. It's why she'd tried to stay away from him all night.

Rather unsuccessfully.

Oh, she'd kept her physical distance, but she'd been mentally distracted. Even with her back to him, she'd known exactly where he was and what he was doing. She'd always been aware of him in that preternatural way and she'd stopped wondering why a long time ago. They were connected.

Unfortunately, that connection was working against her right now.

Her brain might be screaming that everything was *not* okay, but her body didn't seem to give a damn. It just wanted him. Now. Often.

She had a driving need to touch him. To assure herself he was there—and alive. The need bothered her. It seemed like a weakness, one she struggled desperately to conquer. But never did.

Time with her friends had helped to center her, though. She'd really needed those few hours to relax and unwind. To try to forget the tangled mess her life had become.

A tiny voice in her head whispered that a tangled mess was a hell of a lot better than sleepwalking through life, which was what she'd been doing for the last three years.

The problem was, the same voice kept taunting her that the grief and numbness weren't really gone…simply waiting patiently to return.

Beside her, a light clicked on. The warm glow washed over her closed eyelids.

He was standing there, watching her. She didn't need to open her eyes to know it. She could feel his gaze sweep across her and the way her body reacted to his study. Her nipples tightened. Her core ached.

But she didn't move. They both waited, the pressure a physical thing filling the room.

She heard him shift. The air caught in Tatum's lungs. What would he do now? And how would she react? What did she want him to do?

Take the decision out of her hands. Give her mind a break from the round robin of swirling emotions and thoughts. Give her a respite from the confusion, anger, hope and *need* she'd been struggling with since he had walked back into her life.

Tatum tensed, waiting for a caress. Or his mouth.

Instead, he scooped her off the couch into his strong arms.

Her eyelids flashed open, the light blinding her for a moment. Her hands scrambled to find purchase as the couch fell away from her. It felt as if she was floating, and the only thing tethering her to the earth was Evan's arms.

He cradled her against his body, one arm tucked beneath her bent knees and the other a strong band running beneath her shoulders.

She peeked up at him, momentarily stunned. Not because he had picked her up. She wasn't supermodel thin, but she exercised at Sweetheart Sweats on a regular basis. Plus, her husband was a badass with the muscles to prove it. He could easily move her around any way he wanted.

No, it was because of the way he watched her. It made her mouth dry and her eyes prick. Oh, there was lust, too, but mixed with something more. Something she'd missed so much and hadn't let herself see before now.

The love they'd both lost.

"What...what are you doing?"

"Taking my wife to bed," he said in a husky tone.

"I don't..." She had no idea what lie she was going to tell, but the words wouldn't form. She did. She did want. Did need.

His long strides ate up space, carrying her straight to the bedroom they'd been sharing for the past several days.

Gently, he lowered her into a sitting position on the bed and knelt at her feet. His fingers found the fly of her jeans, making quick work of the button and zipper. The backs of his fingers slipped across her skin, his heat making her muscles jump and blood sizzle.

With nothing but a single, glancing touch, she was on fire.

Tatum tried to get control by sucking in a ragged breath, but there was no control to be had.

Evan urged her up onto her feet again. He stayed right where he was, on his knees, his head perfectly aligned with where she needed him.

He didn't glance up at her, but focused squarely on his mission. Hooking fingers into the relaxed waistband of her jeans, he tugged them over her hips, leaving her panties. Not that they were very useful. She could feel the dampness soaking them. They'd been that way since their kiss.

Restless, Tatum shifted on her feet, bringing her satin-covered mound closer to his mouth. But Evan didn't seem to notice. Or at least, he made no move to do anything about it.

The soft puff of his warm breath was pure torture.

Palms spread across her waist, he slowly guided her down onto the edge of the bed. Tears pricked her eyes. It somehow felt like a metaphor for another precarious edge she was balancing on.

Evan tugged her jeans off one leg at a time, and she tried not to shudder when he brushed the slopes of her thighs.

He remained between her spread feet, staring at the floor. She could see the rise and fall of his broken breaths. The stuttering flutter of his pulse at his throat.

And she realized he was trying to get control.

But that's not what she wanted.

For the first time since he'd picked her up, Tatum touched him. Threading her fingers into the silky strands of his black hair, she tugged until his face rose to her.

Their gazes collided, and she sucked in a rough breath. That's what he did to her. He made her forget how to breathe. Forget everything but the way he could make her body burn.

He made no attempt to hide the smoldering hunger lighting up his eyes. Her hold on him tightened. She had to be pulling on his hair, but he didn't even wince. It was as though he couldn't feel anything but his desire for her.

Tatum understood. There wasn't room for anything else.

And still he didn't move. He knelt at her feet, silently begging her to give them what they both wanted. He didn't try to push, yet they knew he could. The kiss they'd shared tonight had demonstrated how fully he could consume her if he wanted.

Tonight wasn't about that kind of unbridled consumption. The first night, she'd goaded him into giving her an orgasm. And their encounter in the workroom at Petals had been all barely banked heat. At every turn, he'd pushed her. Pursued her. Used her physical reactions against her and given her little choice.

Tonight, he was giving her everything.

But that meant she had nothing to hide behind when the night was over and morning rolled back around.

If she told him to leave, Evan would.

But she didn't want him to go. The mere thought of it lodged a pain deep in her chest. It was a familiar ache, one she'd lived with for so long.

Tonight, she wanted it gone.

11

HANDS TWISTED IN his hair, Tatum used her hold to urge him up. Now it was her turn to stare at him. He was gorgeous.

His momentum dislodged her grip on him. Her hands dropped, trailing down his body as he rose, to snag in the waistband of his jeans. Tugging at his shirt, she pushed it up, revealing the tight plane of his abs.

She leaned forward, intending to run her tongue along the peaks and valleys, but the moment she got close, she realized she needed to do something else.

Placing a kiss right above his belly button, she set her forehead against him and wrapped her arms around his hips, just holding him to her.

She breathed in the spicy, clean scent of him. The muscles beneath her contracted. It was his turn to bury his hands deep in her hair, holding hard enough that it should have hurt. But it didn't. She didn't feel any pain, only the relief she'd been desperately holding at bay for days.

Her shoulders shook and an unexpected sob burst through her lips. She tried to smother it, but it was too late.

"Tatum," he breathed, his own voice husky with regret, loneliness and shared pain.

He lifted her head up and stared into her eyes. His thumb brushed slowly across her cheek, spreading a trail of wetness. Until that moment, she hadn't realized she was crying.

"Baby," he whispered. "Please don't."

She shook her head, unable to explain that she couldn't stop.

Gathering her into his arms, he folded them both onto the bed. Her legs were draped across his lap, her face buried deep in his neck. One hand rubbed rhythmically up and down her back. The other held back the fall of her hair, giving him access to rain soothing kisses across her temple, cheek and nose.

"Honey, stop. You're going to make yourself sick."

She curled her fingers harder into the front of his shirt, desperate to hold on.

He murmured to her, incoherent words that probably would have made sense if her mind wasn't caught in the tornado of emotions she'd been denying for days.

Somewhere in the maelstrom, words began to pour from her mouth. All the things she'd sworn she was strong enough to keep buried inside. How devastated she'd been. How hard it had been to keep moving, one day after another, without him. How pissed she'd been at him for dying and leaving her alone. How guilty those thoughts had made her feel afterward. How numb she'd been every day since.

How bone-deep scared she was.

Eventually, she quieted, the flow of words drying to a drip and then stopping all together. He just kept touching her, as though the soft scrape of his callused fingertips over her skin could give her comfort.

The thing was, they did.

The weight of everything she'd been carrying lifted, finally freeing her. Until it was gone, she didn't realize how heavy the burden had been. Or that she'd been carrying it since long before Evan's death…it had started with her mother's illness and had never quite disappeared.

She'd had to be so strong, first for her parents and then for Evan as a military wife. She wasn't immune to the pressure. His job scared her—it had then and it did now. But she refused to be like some of the other wives, letting that fear steer her life. So she'd pushed it down. Pretended it wasn't there.

Until he was gone and she couldn't pretend anymore.

It felt good, finally being able to give the fear words, to share the burden.

And Evan accepted it, taking it on himself without a single complaint.

Tatum had no idea how long they lay there entwined. There was something…profound about the moment. They'd always been close—how could they not be, with everything they'd gone through together?

But this was more.

And eventually, her body became restless, wanting the physical connection as much as the emotional one they'd just shared.

She shifted, feeling the hard ridge of his erection snuggled tight against her hip. And wanted it deep inside her. Needed it more than her next breath.

The room crackled. Or maybe that was the tingle of need flickering beneath her skin.

His mouth found hers. She wanted the heat, the blaze of need to burn through her. Instead, the kiss was soft and sweet with an edge of vulnerability that was nearly her undoing.

He coaxed, teased, gently persuaded her to let him in. With nothing more than the sweep of his enticing tongue, he tore through the defenses she'd been erecting for years.

How had she ever thought to hold him at bay? This was Evan, her best friend long before he'd become her husband. Her rock. The one person who'd always known her better than anyone else—including herself.

Of course, he'd know how to get deep inside.

Tatum sighed, the burst of sound and breath disappearing into the abyss of their shared kiss.

The room tilted and she was on her back. Evan rose above her, somewhere along the way managing to make the shirt he'd been wearing disappear.

She wanted to touch him, to run her fingers along every warm, tanned inch of skin. Her gaze traveled along the ink marking his chest and she couldn't stop the tiny thrill that coursed through her at the memory of its meaning.

Her eyes lowered, drinking in the puckered flesh tucked between two of his ribs. She knew every scar that had marred his beautiful body before leaving for Colombia and this one was definitely new.

Tatum brushed her fingers across his smooth skin, stopping at the jagged proof that something dangerous had ripped through his skin.

Her stomach flipped and a sharp pain stabbed through her own ribs.

"What happened?" she whispered, craning sideways so she could see better.

"Knife," was his terse answer, even as he shifted to block her study.

Tatum sucked in a harsh breath. Jesus, it was so close to his heart.

"How bad?"

"Bad enough."

He might have cut off her view, but he hadn't prevented her from touching. So she continued to let her fingers memorize this new mark on his flesh.

Until he grasped her wrists and locked her hands high above her head with one of his own, holding her immobile beneath him.

"Don't, Tatum. Don't let it ruin this. Don't let it in. Not now. Not tonight."

His deep, dark eyes pleaded with her even as his hips pulsed against hers, driving tiny thrills that curled deliciously through her belly. She heard the need filling his words, not just for her, but for her to let the past go.

She'd never been able to deny him anything. Why had she ever thought she could start now?

Her hands slipped up his skin to rest on the rounded bulges of his shoulders. Tatum nodded, swallowing the rest of the questions her instincts had raised to her tongue.

Just as well, Evan had other uses for it anyway.

Keeping a hold on her wrists, he leaned down and took her mouth. The kiss was soft and subtle, filled with just the right amount of heat and promise. He teased her, exploring her mouth only to pull back and leave her desperate for more.

She chased him, straining against his hold on her and trying to bring their lips back together.

When she couldn't, Tatum settled for whatever else

she could touch. His biceps, bulging against the weight of holding his body steady above hers. The ridge of a rib. The flat disk of a nipple.

She relished the way his body contracted as she grazed her tongue along his skin. She loved the groan that fell from his parted lips. The way his hips, already tight against hers, surged harder, connecting the ridge of his sex with her mound.

Tatum dropped her head, arched her back and undulated against him. She needed more. Was desperate for more. For him.

He finally freed her, trailing his palm down her body, from wrist to shoulder to waist. The caress wasn't gentle, the pressure of his touch demanding. Possessive. As though he was reminding himself just what was his.

And she was stupid to ever think her body was hers. Not when with one touch he could make her yearn and ache.

He braced a palm against the small of her back and lifted her up so he could pull her panties off. Kneeling at her feet, he stared up her body, his eyes full of reverence, joy and worship.

What woman didn't want her husband to look at her that way? As if she was the next best thing to the sun.

But the pressure of her longing quickly became unbearable. "Evan, I need you." Not just her need for him now, but always.

"I know."

No, she didn't think he did, but when his mouth found the inside of her thigh and brushed hot, wet kisses across her skin, her thoughts scattered and she no longer had the capacity to explain.

Not now.

He was shattering her. And her defenses.

Without a word of argument, he was systematically stripping her bare. Taking away every defense and rationalization she'd tried to use to protect herself and her heart.

They were useless. As she'd known, deep down somewhere, they would be. But she'd had to try.

Her fingertips played across his skin, touching every inch she could reach. Reclaiming it as surely as he was. Their marriage had been an equal partnership and she refused to let it be anything else tonight.

Coaxing him higher, Tatum spread her thighs wide in an invitation they both recognized. Evan didn't hesitate to accept it.

With one quick surge, he entered her, sliding all the way home.

Heaven. Tatum's eyelids fluttered against the overwhelming sensation. Perfect. He was perfect. They were absolutely perfect together.

She wanted him to let the fever and madness take over, surrender to the passion. But he didn't do that. Instead, he stilled, wrapped his arms around her body and pulled her tight into his embrace.

He surrounded her. Was everywhere. His scent and skin and strength. She wasn't exactly sure where he stopped and she began. Not anymore.

He simply held her, long enough so she could feel the subtle throb of his pulse, in his sex buried inside her, at the arch of his throat and in his wrists planted heavy against her back. Or maybe that was the beat of her own need she felt.

Either way, it was maddening, beautiful and soul destroying.

The vulnerability of the moment welled up inside

her, making her restless. She shifted, trying to find a release. Relief. But he wouldn't let her move.

Instead, he whispered in her ear, "Shh, I've got you, Tatum. I promise, I'll always be here."

"Oh, God," she moaned, unable to hide or fight the tide of emotion crashing through her.

And that was the moment he finally started to move, adding a searing pleasure to the mix. It was more than she could fight. More than she could handle.

More than she'd ever experienced in her life, which was saying a lot considering how close they'd been before he was gone.

How could something so devastating bring them closer together?

But Tatum didn't have the time or mental capacity to figure out the answer.

Not when the tension in her body was building quickly to the point of explosion. She could feel it, that edge racing toward her, like the exhilaration and joy of opening her Mustang wide and screaming into the wind. Only better. So much better.

Because she wasn't alone.

Evan was right there with her, stroke for delicious stroke. She could feel his body winding tighter and tighter. Hear the ragged exhalation of his breath, feel the gush of it against her overheated skin. The pressure of his hands held her steady and grounded her even as her body prepared to soar.

And then it was there, too powerful to hold back.

The orgasm broke over her, but in the middle of that vortex of unbelievable pleasure, Evan experienced it with her.

Everything else faded away, but he was there. The gush of her name streaming from his lips, reverence filling the single word. The jagged pulse of his hips against hers as he took every last speck of pleasure for himself and gave it back to her tenfold.

His fingers clenched, pressing her hard against his chest. It should have hurt, but didn't. She wanted to be that close. Would have crawled inside his skin if it had been physically possible. She'd never felt so connected.

His lips brushed across her skin, raining butterfly kisses wherever he could touch. A shudder rocked her. He rolled, pulling out, but somehow managed to keep their bodies tangled.

They lay together for a while; Tatum wasn't entirely certain how long. She traced random patterns on his skin, her head tucked protectively beneath his chin. His hands played in her hair, sifting through it and spreading the strands across the pillow.

They were quiet. Content. At least she thought so until he asked, "Where's your ring?"

Tatum's body went hard with tension. It wasn't necessarily the question, just the unexpected nature of it blasting in and obliterating the soft comfort she'd been basking in.

"I have it."

"Where?"

Without looking, Tatum pointed across the room to the jewelry box sitting atop her dresser.

Tucked as she was against him, she felt the stuttered rise and fall of his chest as he pulled in a deep breath. Was he building courage or preparing for some pain?

"When did you take it off?"

Maybe a little bit of both.

"When I came to Sweetheart. It felt…like the right time. I was building a new life. No one here knew I was married and it was easier that way. Here there were no looks of pity or reminders of our life together."

Although that wasn't precisely true. She could tell herself that none of the restaurants, businesses or furniture in her house carried reminders of Evan, but she hadn't needed him to share those places and things for him to leave an imprint.

She'd imagined him at the pub, watching a game with her and her friends on a Saturday night. Or sharing a meal over candlelight at the Speckled Hen. She'd purposely bought a new bed when she'd moved into this house, but that hadn't stopped the midnight fantasies of him sharing it with her.

Reaching behind him, Evan grasped the hand that had been playing across his back, her left one, and brought it between them. Bending his head, he let his lips trail across her ring finger, right where her wedding ring should have been.

He didn't pressure her. Didn't ask her to get out of bed, retrieve the reminder of their life together, and place it back where it belonged.

She knew he wanted to. Wanted the obvious symbol that she was taken back on her finger.

But he didn't demand.

He simply said, "I hope one day you'll let me put it back."

Her heart melted. A part of her was ready to vault up, grab the ring and ask him to do just that. But something held her back.

Caution. Fear. She wasn't sure, but whatever it was, it kept her silent and still, burying the fantasy of what that might mean—a future she didn't truly believe they could ever share.

Finally opening herself up to him had only increased her potential for heartache when it all went wrong.

12

THE NEXT DAY crept past, completely uneventful and yet somehow…wrong. Tatum was restless, an uncomfortable sensation chipping away at the base of her spine.

All the muscles in her body were useless. As if they were falling down on a job none of them were aware they were supposed to be doing.

Evan walked to the front door of her store, flipped the sign to Closed and bolted the lock. He shut off the small lamps in the display area, which highlighted the pottery and glass vases from local artists. He double-checked that the cooler was shut and all the arrangements inside were fresh enough for another day.

Tatum watched his movements. He barely made a sound as he slipped through her space, almost as if he didn't disturb the air. She wondered if he was actually a ghost. The panic she kept fighting off surfaced, stronger than ever. But she shook the thought away. A ghost couldn't touch her the way Evan did.

It was a little scary how quickly they'd fallen into a routine. And how easily he'd taken over some of her normal, everyday responsibilities.

They moved together, around each other, communicating with nothing more than a look or raised eyebrow.

It was comfortable. And comforting.

But wrong. As much as her heart screamed at her to accept what she had while she had it, Tatum couldn't let the encroaching unease go.

Turning away, she disappeared into the back of the store to clean up her worktable. She was in the middle of sweeping little bits of leaves, stems and ribbon from the floor when a loud clatter sounded from the other side of her back door.

Dropping the broom and dustpan with a sharp bang, Tatum bolted toward the noise. There were voices—clear, loud and distressed.

The alley at the back of Petals ran the entire length of Main Street. Businesses and homes on either side backed onto it. It was where she parked her delivery van for easy loading and unloading.

Before she could stop and think, Tatum was out the door, racing for whoever was in trouble.

She hadn't realized how dark it had gotten—during the last fifteen minutes she'd been in the back room, every last speck of daylight had faded. It was the one thing she hated about winter, even if South Carolina didn't often suffer the other effects she was used to—such as piles and piles of snow.

She could barely make out silhouettes at the end of the alley. At least two people. No, maybe three. They were huddled together over something.

One of them sprang back, letting out a yell that Tatum didn't quite understand.

Was the shadow on the ground another person? Someone hurt? Were they hollering for help?

Sprinting as quickly as her legs would carry her,

Tatum barreled headlong for the cluster. But her strides faltered when the group scattered, at least two of them running in her direction.

They waved their hands. It took Tatum several moments, as they moved steadily closer, to realize the figures belonged to a group of teenage boys. And they were hotfooting it away from where they'd been standing.

And then the world exploded with loud pops and bangs, bright colors that forced her eyes shut, although she could still see the starbursts across her closed lids.

Something sizzled across her calf. She yelped in surprise and pain, dropping to the ground, clutching her leg. What the hell! Had she been shot?

No, guns didn't make bright colors.

Something heavy slammed onto her back, driving her into a crumpled ball on the ground. All the air whooshed from her lungs.

"Stay down," a voice commanded in her ear before the weight disappeared.

Tatum glanced up quickly to see Evan disappearing into the melee in front of her. Smoke. Chaos. Noise.

Her brain scrambled to fit together the pieces of the picture in front of her.

Fireworks. That's what the bursts of color were, but they definitely hadn't been aimed at the sky. Or maybe they had been at one point, but they sure hadn't ended up there.

Her leg throbbed. Tatum took in the black streak scorched through the leg of her jeans. The material around it smoldered. Wrapping her hand in the sleeve of her shirt, Tatum slammed it down over the curling wisps, smothering whatever heat was left. She hissed at the pain, but she didn't move her hand.

When she was certain her jeans weren't about to burst into flame, Tatum tried to orient herself in the smoky alley. To her right another figure lay crumpled on the ground.

The artificial screams and whistles were slowing, but Tatum still didn't want to stand up. Knowing her luck, as soon as she did the fireworks' finale would hit...her.

Pushing up to her elbows, she crawled—staying as low as possible—the few feet over to check on whoever had hit the ground beside her.

Both arms crossed protectively over his head, the boy lay with his face buried deep in the gravel and grass. Had he passed out? Was he injured? Breathing? It was so dark she couldn't tell, and the occasional bursts of light weren't helping. In fact, each time her eyes started to adjust to the low light, another rocket would go off and blind her all over again.

Placing a hand on the middle of his back, Tatum sighed in relief when she felt the boy's ribs expand and contract. He shifted, rolling up onto his hip, and she got a partial look at his face.

"Will Marshall, what were you guys thinking?" Tatum pushed at his raised shoulder, silently telling him to roll onto his back so she could look for hidden injuries. "Your mother is going to kill you."

His face crumpled and she thought he might start crying. She couldn't remember how old he was, maybe thirteen or fourteen. Stuck between a kid and a man. And his reaction proved it, although Tatum had to give him credit for fighting back the tears. He bit down on his trembling bottom lip. As she watched, his expression hardened.

"Yes, ma'am, she is. But I guess I deserve it."

Oh, hell. "We'll see. As long as none of you are hurt…" Tatum's voice trailed off, unwilling to make promises she couldn't keep. She'd certainly pulled enough crap of her own growing up. At least until she'd had to take on the responsibility of holding her family together.

There was a part of her that wanted these boys to keep their childhood, even if that sometimes included pulling boneheaded and dangerous pranks. It wasn't as if this town didn't have plenty of stories like that to go around, probably half of them featuring one or all of these boys' fathers.

"Are you okay?" she asked. "Were you hit?"

"I'm fine."

Tatum nodded, accepting the small trill of relief washing through her.

"But you're not." The boy nodded to her leg.

"It's nothing. These jeans were ready for the trash bin anyway."

Will gave her a strange look, but didn't argue.

Flashes of pink, gold and green sparks showered several feet away, but she hadn't heard any more rockets going off. Gingerly pushing up to a crouch, Tatum looked around, but all she could see were the ghosts of fireworks past bursting across her vision.

Deciding the coast was clear enough, she said, "Stay here," to Will and then headed farther down the alley.

Smoke choked the already cramped space, obscuring her vision more than the cloud-covered night. Up ahead, she heard a yelp and a gurgle. Her heart hitched in her chest and her stomach dropped to her toes.

Please don't let one of the boys be seriously hurt.

Racing through the fog, Tatum skidded to a halt.

Instead of what she'd expected—to find a boy crumpled on the ground nursing a face that had been burned off, which would have been horrific—what she found was ten times worse.

Evan's hands were wrapped around two skinny throats. The boys' backs were pressed against a wooden fence, the slats groaning beneath the force of their combined weight. Tatum was afraid the whole thing would collapse behind them.

Her husband was at least a foot and a half taller than both boys and almost double their width. From her vantage point behind them, Tatum might have missed the second boy, if she hadn't noticed Evan's hands clamped around both throats.

He was leaning into them, pinning them beneath his heavily muscled body.

Their eyes bugged out, round with fear. Their toes barely touched the ground, scrabbling around to try and find better purchase to ease the pressure of his palm against their windpipes.

Evan growled at them. Tatum heard the even cadence of his voice, but couldn't understand the words.

Jesus, this wasn't good.

Racing up to them, Tatum tried to wedge herself between Evan and the boys, but there wasn't enough room. She settled for clamping a fist tight around Evan's wrist.

"Let them go," she said in a cool, commanding tone.

Without sparing her a glance, he said, "No."

"Evan, look at me." The words were a plea, but she tried to keep them from sounding that way. That weakness wouldn't help anyone right now.

When he didn't respond, she said it again, this time adding a whip to her voice. "Look. At. Me."

Slowly, his head swiveled, his gaze colliding with hers.

Tatum sucked in a sharp breath, but tried to keep any other reaction from her face.

Everything about him was hard, his mouth, jaw, eyes. They were...*dead* wasn't the right word, but as damn close as they could get. Almost as if he'd been given a death sentence long ago and was merely living out the remainder of his time.

This person wasn't the man she'd fallen in love with and married.

This was the stranger who'd been lurking beneath the surface since he'd returned.

Ruthless, deadly, dangerous, vicious.

Swallowing, Tatum tried to push those thoughts from her head.

"Let them go, Evan. They did something stupid, but you know this isn't right." She tipped her head sideways to where he held them immobilized.

"You could have been hurt."

"I wasn't."

Her calf chose that moment to throb unbearably, but Tatum ignored it. Nothing a little ointment and bandages couldn't fix so she didn't feel bad for the lie. Really, it wasn't one.

"Why the hell did you run out here, Tatum? You had no idea what kind of danger you were dashing headlong into."

Cutting her eyes sideways, Tatum noticed his hold on the boys had eased up. One of them moved to squirm, meaning to take advantage of the slack, but Tatum shook her head.

"I wasn't in danger, Evan. I thought someone was hurt. I wanted to help."

He studied her. The harsh angles that had sharpened his features eased, giving her a glimpse of the man she loved.

With the same sudden shock of the fireworks going off, Evan dropped his hold on the boys and transferred it to her.

His arms were hard bands around her middle. He crushed her to him, forcing out what little breath she had left.

Gazing over his shoulder, she watched the boys—Ben Dorian and Gil Southern—crumple to the ground. They both stared up at her, their gazes a mix of relief, regret and pure fear.

"Why don't you boys go on home," she suggested in as soft a voice as she could manage.

It was all the urging they needed. Their legs were unsteady, but somehow managed to hold them up as they bolted away.

She'd have to make a few phone calls tonight. Even if she felt sympathy for the boys, their parents needed to know what happened. And she wasn't only talking about the fireworks.

The minute the boys were clear, her own battered body gave out. Beneath the weight of Evan's embrace, she sagged, but she didn't hit the ground.

For the first time she noticed a knot of people who'd gathered at the far end of the alley. But Evan didn't give her a chance to talk to them before he scooped her into his arms, somehow managing to slam her injured leg against the hard bone of his hip. A mangled cry of pain slipped through her lips and he cursed.

Gentling his hold, he shifted her higher. The pain she'd been ignoring swirled up and threatened to pull her down. The back door of Petals stood wide open, light spilling out into the cool night. Evan didn't bother to close it behind them as he strode through. Instead, he plopped her rear on top of her worktable, easing her back until she was stretched out on top of it.

A low, rumbling growl rolled through his throat when he got his first good look at her leg.

His accusing gaze cut up to her. "Not hurt, huh?"

"Not really," she said, but she could hear the shudder of pain in her words.

He scowled, grasped the blackened hole on her jeans and pulled. With a loud rip the material tore straight down to the thick band at the hem.

With heavy hands on her shoulders, Evan gave her no choice but to lie back and roll onto her hip, allowing him full access to the angry burn running along the side of her leg.

Tatum twisted, trying to see, but his body blocked her.

"Where's your first-aid kit?"

Tatum pointed to a cupboard in the corner where she kept supplies that she rarely used. Giving her a sharp look, Evan strode away, stopping to grab several towels from the stack she kept handy to clean up spills. Going to the sink, he ran one under the water, wringing it out before gingerly placing the towel on her leg.

"This should help cool it off."

The contact stung like hell, but he was right; almost immediately the heat radiating up and down her leg subsided.

He rummaged in the first-aid kit and pulled out a roll of gauze.

"There should be some antibiotic ointment in there," she said.

Without looking up at her, he shook his head. "Not supposed to put ointment on a burn."

She wasn't sure about that, but wasn't about to argue with him. Not right this minute, anyway. Of the two of them, only one had received battlefield medical training, and it wasn't her.

He checked her compress, went to the sink, soaked another towel and changed it. After that was finished, he simply stood next to her, staring down at his hands folded together on the table beside her hip.

Tatum placed her hand over his. He didn't move or acknowledge her touch at all, which only made panic bubble deep inside her chest.

"Evan, talk to me," she whispered. "What happened in Colombia? No more half-truths or evasions. I need to know. Not for me, but for you."

TATUM'S WORDS SPUN through his mind, mixing with the memories that threatened to consume him. Not just from his time in Colombia, but from tonight.

The looks on those boys' faces...

Dread rolled up the back of his throat, threatening to cut off his air supply.

They were teenagers, and he'd held them up by their necks. He could have easily squeezed the life out of them. Had felt his fingers flex and tighten with instinct—kill or be killed.

He wasn't entirely certain he could have stopped if Tatum hadn't tried to wedge herself between them. Her scent, her voice, her touch had pulled him back from the brink.

But she wouldn't always be there.

And if he couldn't control himself, did he deserve to ask her to be?

The memory of waking up that first night with

her pinned beneath him joined the toxic mix inside his head.

He was barbaric, driven by the most animalistic urges. He was dangerous to anyone who got close, maybe Tatum in particular.

One thing he knew was that if anything ever happened to her he'd absolutely fall apart. Especially if he was the cause of her injury.

Maybe he really did need to take Lock's advice and talk to someone. But right now his first priority was taking care of Tatum.

Brushing his fingers softly over the compress covering her leg, Evan tried to swallow the sick sensation churning in his stomach. Hell, he was struggling right now and all she had was a fairly small second-degree burn.

He didn't deserve her. That was the bottom line. And maybe it was time for her to realize that, too.

Taking off the compress, he lifted her leg, bending it at the knee so he would have space to wrap the gauze around her calf. This would be easier if he could keep his hands busy.

"You want to know what happened?" he asked, his voice gruff.

"Yes." Her answer was simple, but there was no way she could know what she was really asking for. Hell, he'd lived it and he didn't want those memories anymore.

"I don't think you do, Tatum."

Grasping his hands, she stopped him mid twist. He shook his head, realizing he'd wound over half the roll of gauze around her leg. With a grunt, he dropped the rest of it to the table and watched it roll to the floor, leaving a tail of white in its wake.

She squeezed, probably trying to give him support or encouragement. It wouldn't be enough.

Slowly, Evan's gaze traveled the length of her gorgeous legs. Legs that just last night had been wrapped tight around his waist while he was buried deep inside her body. If he'd known it was going to be the last time, he would have…savored.

Had she had similar thoughts after they told her he was dead?

Swallowing a sudden lump in his throat, he forced his gaze to continue up, over her thighs and hips. Waist and chest. The smooth column of her throat. Those perfect, pouting lips that could pour out such wit and sarcasm even as they blinded with the brightest smile.

He wanted to linger there. To lean in and kiss her so hard they'd both remember the taste and feel forever. But he didn't. Instead, he forced himself to continue up to her emerald eyes.

Tonight they weren't quite as bright as he liked to see them. She couldn't hide the residual, dulling edge of pain, not from her wound, but the memory of losing him. Or the fear. He knew she didn't want him to see, but he could.

He'd always been able to see her, maybe especially the things she tried to hide from the world behind a facade of bravado and strength.

It hurt that he was the cause, when he'd promised her a long time ago he'd be the one to protect and support her.

"Trust me," she murmured.

"Always," he answered without hesitation. "You're not the problem here, Tatum."

He didn't have to finish for her to understand. She

knew what he meant, what he couldn't bring himself to say.

"Then let me trust you."

"You shouldn't."

She shook her head, her eyes taking on a fierce glitter he recognized all too well. She was gearing up to take on the world. Or at least his demons.

"Dammit, Evan. You can't walk back into my life, blow it apart, beg me to let you in and then hold me at arm's length. That isn't a life or a relationship. It isn't enough. Before, it might have been. But it isn't anymore."

She was right. He knew it, and yet…

"Fine," he said. "You want to know that I killed a man? Several men? That I held a gun to a guy's temple and pulled the trigger? Watched his blood and brains splatter on the wall? He was a husband and a father.

"Or that I put drugs in the hands of children. Knowing they'd be selling to other kids. Getting people hooked. Ruining their lives before they had a chance to really live. Probably condemning them to an early grave before they hit sixteen.

"That I watched as men beat their women and couldn't do anything to stop it, not without blowing the entire operation? That I had to play God and choose whose life was worth saving and who we could afford to lose as a casualty in a war the rest of the world had no idea we were waging?"

Evan heard his voice crack, but not even that could stop the flow of words once they'd started. It was as if every sin he'd ever committed had been bottled up inside and suddenly freed. They erupted like rotten champagne, spewing sewage over everything.

"Every night, for three years, I slept with a gun beneath my pillow, safety off and my finger on the trigger. My other hand was inches away from the knife strapped to my thigh. I didn't get a single moment of rest."

Evan peered down at his hands. In a small corner of his head, he registered that they were shaking, but the vision didn't compute. He didn't feel the tremble. How could he, when his body was completely numb? Disconnected.

Until she touched him.

Somewhere along the way, his legs must have given out. Or maybe he decided to sit down. Either way, his ass was on the floor and his back was pressed against the cabinets that ran beneath the sink.

And she was sprawled right beside him.

She shouldn't be down here, in the muck with him.

Evan tried to grasp her arms, pull them both up off the floor, but he couldn't do it. Not only were his arms and legs less than cooperative, but so was Tatum. She wouldn't budge.

In fact, she weighed him down, crawling right up into his lap.

The warmth of her body pressed against him. For a second, he reveled in the power of it. The cleansing heat of her. It would be so easy to let her give that to him.

But it was wrong. This was wrong. She shouldn't be this close to him.

Evan tried to shove her off, but that didn't work. Not when she wound her arms around his shoulders and simply hung on.

Burying her face in the crook of his neck, she pressed cool lips on his skin. Over and over again, her mouth touched anything she could reach. There wasn't heat, at least not the conflagration that usually consumed them. The warmth that blazed wherever she touched was purer. Soothing. Understanding. Accepting.

Even after everything he'd just told her.

And that's what gave him the strength to finally push her away.

Or at least try.

He got them both standing. He reached behind his head and peeled her fingers away. Unfortunately, the moment he got one hand off, the other seemed to reattach—to his waistband, over his biceps or around his hip. It didn't matter what he did, she was like a starfish, suction-cupped to his body, refusing to let go.

Finally frustrated beyond reason, Evan roared, "Didn't you hear a word I said?"

"Yes. Every one."

Leaning into him, she plastered her body against his, bringing them together, from shoulders to knees.

He realized the trembling filling his limbs wasn't entirely his. Tatum shook, too, fine tremors racking her from head to toe.

"And most of the ones you didn't say. You aren't a monster, Evan. You couldn't be."

Oh, how wrong she was. "I could. I am."

"No, you made tough decisions in a terrible situation. I'm sure the man you killed would have killed you, because you've never been the kind of man to hurt in cold blood, and I don't believe anything—*anything*—could change that. Change you."

"I did change, Tatum. I'm a different man than the one who left you three years ago."

Her soft palms bracketed his face, forcing him to look at her, stare into her soul. And bare his own. But she already saw his fears and doubts. What else was there left to hide?

"Yes, you are different. Maybe you're a little harder. Your muscles certainly are," she said, the hint of a smile tugging at her lips.

Was she making a joke? Now? Evan was bewildered and...strangely proud. Tatum was strong, always had been. It wasn't often he was surprised, but she'd just managed to do it.

"But the core of the man you are, the slightly awkward teenager I fell in love with, the honorable soldier he grew into and the tenacious, strong husband who always protected me and anyone else who needed it... that hasn't changed. And never will."

God, for the first time since the words began spewing from his mouth, Evan really looked at Tatum. He'd been afraid to, certain that what he was telling her would drive any hope of her loving him again straight into the ground.

But it wasn't true.

The love she'd always given freely, but had been suppressing since his return, was finally back on display.

How was that possible?

Evan didn't know and mostly didn't care.

She wasn't pushing him away. In fact, she was actively trying to draw him closer. And it wasn't pity or obligation, which he never would have accepted.

It was so much more.

A weight that he'd been carrying around for three long years slipped from his shoulders. The relief was... exquisite and a little unnerving. He'd gotten so used to shouldering it.

"I was so afraid, Tatum. Afraid that I wouldn't be

able to shed the skin I'd been wearing. That it had become a part of me, especially the things I hated."

"Never," she said, the single word reminding him of a mother lion protecting her cubs—territorial and dangerous in her own right.

"I just…sometimes those instincts kick in and I can't stop them. Like that first night in your guest bedroom. Or tonight."

"You didn't do anything either time, Evan."

"I could have."

"You didn't."

His fingertips slipped along the slope of her cheeks. "Because you were there."

Before the words were out, Tatum was already shaking her head.

"I had nothing to do with that. It was all you."

"I think you underestimate your calming influence." His mouth twisted into a smile, and it felt a little rusty and stiff, but somehow good. Great, actually.

She snorted. "No one has ever accused me of being a calming influence. Are you sure you didn't get hit in the head by a bottle rocket and have your brain rattled?"

Working his fingers deep into the silky strands of her hair, Evan tilted her head and held her still.

"No. You're exactly what I need, Tatum. You've always been what I need. Hoping I'd come back to you was the only thing that got me through that hell."

He expected…something. Joy, happiness, maybe a touch of humble pride. What he didn't expect was a frown to tug at the edges of her mouth.

But almost before it registered, her expression was smooth again.

"I saw you tonight, Evan. You knew exactly how

tight to hold to inflict a healthy dose of fear into those boys without actually hurting. And you were doing that long before I jumped in. You were in control—of yourself and the situation."

Wrapping her hands around his wrists, Tatum held on to him.

"Just like that first night. I had the wind knocked out of me because you surprised me, but I was never in danger."

She leaned forward, punctuating her words with a drilling stare. "I was never in any danger and my body and brain knew it."

"Your body just liked being pinned beneath mine. I might have been half out of it for most of the experience, but I was awake enough at the end to remember the aftermath of that kiss. And the way your nipples puckered."

He allowed a playful smile to dance across his lips and dropped his gaze to her chest. Yep, the tight buds of her nipples tempted him to bend down and suck one deep inside his mouth. With a single raised eyebrow, he silently drove home what he meant.

Tatum huffed. "You're missing the point."

No, he wasn't, but he wasn't sure he was ready to accept it.

She might trust him, but he didn't trust himself. Yet. But maybe she was right and all he needed was time. Distance away from the experience that had sent his life spinning irrevocably off course.

And he knew exactly how he wanted to spend that time.

Scooping her into his arms, Evan headed for the back door.

"What are you doing?"

Flipping off the lights, he plunged Petals into the dark, and took advantage of the cover for a sneak attack, claiming her mouth in a deep, drugging kiss.

"I'm taking my wife home."

13

FOR THE FIRST time since he had walked out of the jungle in Colombia, Evan finally felt on solid ground. And it was all because of Tatum.

He had his wife back. The ever-present knot in his stomach had eased.

There were no more secrets. He'd shared everything, and she hadn't turned away from him in disgust. He'd felt the difference last night as they'd made love. The way it had been before. As if they were connected, knew each other from the inside out in a way only a husband and wife could.

He'd missed that connection so damn much.

It felt unbelievably good to have it back.

Of course, it didn't hurt that Tatum was walking around with a perpetual smile tugging at her lips. She wasn't the kind of woman who mooned about; she was action and fire. It did something to him to know he was the reason she'd gone all soft, that he had put that dreamy expression on her face.

It made him feel special and strong.

The same contentment and happiness bubbled up

in his chest. He was invincible today. Nothing could dampen his spirits.

Snagging Tatum's waist as she walked past the counter, he pulled her to his chest, nuzzling at the warm, fragrant curve of her neck.

"Stop," she scolded, pushing halfheartedly at his hands.

He heard a snicker from the display area, but ignored it.

"We have customers, Evan."

He liked the way she'd said *we*, without even thinking about it. In her mind, Petals had become theirs, not just hers.

He wanted that.

Surprisingly, he'd enjoyed the last week running the store with her. Who would have expected him to enjoy the low-key, gently paced world of selling flowers?

Although, if any of the guys, especially Lock, ever saw him here…he'd never hear the end of it.

But maybe it was time to consider a career change. Something a little quieter.

He had to admit, he'd been skeptical at first, but Sweetheart had grown on him. He could see staying here, settling down.

And he really liked Tatum's friends.

It was too soon to throw all of this at her, but maybe tonight, over candlelight and wine, he'd nonchalantly mention his thoughts on retiring from the military and gauge her response. Ask her again about returning his ring to her finger.

Taking a teasing nip at her throat, he said, "Surely, our customers have seen a man kiss his wife before. If not, I'm happy to give them an education."

An exasperated sigh escaped her lips, but her body

relaxed in his arms and she stopped trying to push him away.

He'd only meant to tease her a bit, but the moment she melted against him, instinct took over. His mouth roamed, filling up on the salty-sweet taste of her skin.

"I don't suppose he has a brother?" an amused female voice asked from their left.

"Nope," Tatum sang.

Evan stopped his roaming long enough to say, "They broke the mold when they made me."

Tatum groaned. "Thank God. Could you imagine two of him?"

She squirmed out of his arms and went to help the customer, ringing up the gorgeous arrangement of white roses, lilies—and several other things he still couldn't identify—in a red glass vase.

As soon as the woman walked out the door, Tatum turned to him, preemptively striking down his intention to pick back up where they'd left off.

Hands held out in front of her, Tatum said, "You're going to take me to lunch. But before you do, we're going to run by the bank. I haven't made a deposit in a couple of days."

Disappointment swamped him. But he didn't let it get him down long. He could be persuasive…his lunchtime plans were much more enjoyable than hers.

Unfortunately, he'd barely made a move toward her before she was derailing that plan.

"Don't even think about it, mister." Tatum moved around to the other side of the table, pointing a finger at the front of the store. "Flip the sign and lock the door. I'll meet you at the car."

Evan sized up the distance between them and Tatum's clear path to the back door. She was fast, but he was faster. He'd bet he could get around the table before she made it out the door.

"Uh-uh," she said, shaking her head slowly in a warning his body was desperately urging him to ignore. "Later. I promise. If you're good."

Giving her a wolfish smile, Evan's voice went husky with dark promise. "You know you don't want me to be good, Tatum."

She couldn't suppress the shiver that rocked her body, but still she didn't cave. Instead, she walked backward with small, deliberate steps, closing the distance between her and the door.

He couldn't win.

Raking her with a heated gaze, Evan watched her movements, enjoying the view since it looked as though that was all he was going to get. When her back hit the door, he finally turned and went to close up the front.

Tatum was already sitting in the passenger seat waiting for him when he jogged out. The key was in the ignition, the car idling.

She was flipping through the deposit tucked into the dark blue bank bag, although he wasn't certain why. She'd meticulously prepared it last night so he knew it was perfect.

There were a couple of banks in Sweetheart, but according to Tatum, most of the original families used the one at the end of Main Street. It had been there over a hundred years, the building itself one of the oldest in the city.

It was an institution, and since Petal's previous owner had kept all her accounts there, Tatum had chosen to do the same.

"You can stay in the car if you want," she offered as he pulled into a spot.

Last night might not have ended in his worst nightmare—the guys from Colombia finding him and putting a bullet through Tatum's heart as payback—but he was still reluctant to let her out of his sight.

"No, I'll come in."

She shrugged, gathered her purse and tucked the bank bag beneath her arm. Without waiting for him, she strode ahead. And he couldn't help but watch the way her hips swayed. She was trying to kill him. The question was, was she doing it on purpose?

Three steps inside the front door, Evan slammed into Tatum's body. She rocked on her feet. His arm flashed out around her waist to steady her.

It took only a few seconds to register that her body had gone completely stiff. "What are you...?" he started to ask, but the words died in his throat as his gaze finally moved to take in the room in front of them.

People lying face-first on the floor.

A masked man stood five feet away, the yawning mouth of a gun pointed straight at Tatum's chest.

Instinct kicked in. His first concern was Tatum. His gaze racing around the bank, Evan realized the guy was alone.

In a single blur of motion, he pushed her out of the way, in the direction of a desk that would provide a barrier between her and any flying bullets. Stepping forward, he used his body to give her cover and made himself a target instead.

His teeth clacked together so hard the reverberation rattled through his head, but he didn't register the pain.

"Down on the ground," the guy ordered, the mask covering his face muffling his words.

All Evan could see were the man's eyes, cold and

dead. He was covered from head to toe, wearing a long-sleeved plaid flannel shirt, pants that bagged around his waist and sneakers so old Evan would bet there was at least one hole in the sole.

In a quick moment of assessment, Evan realized this guy was done. With rules. With life. He didn't care, had nothing else to live for.

And that made him dangerous.

Evan had stared down men like this before. Rules like "thou shalt not kill" only worked if the person threatening murder cared what society thought. Or what the repercussions would be—now and later.

Once the veneer of civility was stripped away, the only thing left was survival. And this guy had clearly been surviving on his own for a while.

He didn't have any morals left.

Evan had seen men pushed to that point. He'd seen men born that way. It didn't matter how they had gotten there, only that the only ones who could stop them from doing something horrible were men like Evan.

Men who still knew right from wrong.

In a flash, Evan realized all the fears he'd been holding on to—that deep down his three years in Colombia had pushed him to become a man just like this one—were unfounded.

He'd never wave a gun in a room full of innocent men, women and children. The men he'd killed had been malicious and dangerous. Killing them had probably saved countless lives.

Knowing that didn't quite wash the blood from his hands, but it certainly made it easier to live with.

He took a single step forward, trying to make himself as big a target as possible.

From his left, Tatum whispered his name, but he didn't move his focus off the man in front of him.

He didn't even glance at the gun. Didn't have to in order to know it was pointed straight at him. The gun wasn't what would hurt him. It was the man holding it that would decide whether the trigger was pulled.

So he kept his gaze trained solely on the two hard chips of the bank robber's eyes and waited for the telltale sign.

"Stop," the gunman yelled, but Evan ignored him.

The guy shifted, the gun moving with him. Evan saw his opening and took it.

He leaped forward, slamming into the guy, grabbing at his wrist and pushing the gun up in an arc toward the ceiling.

A loud crack filled his head and a sharp ache rocketed through his body. But he didn't stop his forward momentum.

Something snapped. Evan heard it and felt the echo of it jolt up his arm. The guy screamed. The gun clattered to the floor, skidding across the slippery tile. Evan's weight and power drove them both to the ground, but that wasn't enough.

Rearing his arm back, Evan put every ounce of strength he had behind the blow he drove into the guy's stomach. A strangled sound erupted from his parted lips. Another punch landed just under the sharp edge of his jaw. The gunman's head snapped backward, banging against the hard floor.

And he stopped struggling.

Evan stilled, staring at the man spread limply across the floor. He was simply unconscious, his chest continuing to rise and fall with even breaths.

Where was the rage he'd felt last night when he'd

had those teenagers pinned against the alley fence? It had been overwhelming, almost more than he could fight against. Now, when Tatum had really been in serious trouble…nothing.

Well, not nothing. Relief. Everyone was safe.

Around him people stirred, finally standing up. Evan rolled the guy onto his stomach, wrenched his arms behind his back and used his belt to tie them in place.

The manager, a man dressed in a suit and wearing a shell-shocked expression, rushed up beside him. *Thank you*s poured out. People slapped him on the back. A small child cried.

And the world went a little gray around the edges.

"Tatum," he said, not sure if the word was a question or a statement.

Sitting back on his heels, Evan let his gaze roam across the faces surrounding him until he finally found hers several feet away.

She was staring at him. And the horror filling her beautiful emerald eyes had the panic he should have felt five minutes ago swelling hard inside him.

The low drone of approaching sirens registered. His mouth opened, although he wasn't sure what to say, not that it mattered. Before he could get a single word out, she whirled away.

She left him there, sitting on his ass in the middle of the bank, an armed robber trussed up beside him and blood rolling down his side.

14

OH, GOD. TATUM stumbled out of the bank. Her palms scraped against something hard. Brick? No, the sidewalk. When had she fallen?

Her knees smarted. But that pain was nothing compared to the gaping wound in the center of her chest.

She couldn't breathe.

Reaching up, she tried to ease the pressure, pushing on her ribs. Maybe then her lungs would work.

But they didn't.

Holy hell, the blood.

It was all she could see. That river of bright red leaking down Evan's side to pool in a puddle on the floor. In her head, there were twinkling Christmas lights, though logically she knew that couldn't be right.

But her brain was twisting things. Overlaying the memory of her father onto Evan as he'd crumpled to the floor.

There was so much blood.

She was going to lose him. She couldn't lose him. Not again.

Panic welled up inside her, forcing out everything else.

The scene played over and over. Evan pushing her

out of the way, stepping right in front of that gun. *Right in front.* Stupid, noble, self-sacrificing, *goddamn* man.

Her chest hitched. A ragged sound leaked through her lips.

The way he'd moved toward the gunman, making himself an even bigger target.

Tatum had never been so afraid in her entire life.

But Evan, he'd been...calm. Accepting. He'd known there was a huge possibility he was going to get shot, killed, and he didn't even stop to think twice about putting himself in that position.

Because that's the kind of man he was.

And Tatum loved him for that.

But...the blood.

And the sound of the gun going off. She hadn't heard the gun her father had used, not really, but in her nightmares...she'd seen the devastation left behind.

The bullet may as well have ripped through her own body. It had certainly felt as if it had.

She'd watched as all color had drained out of Evan's face. And still he'd kept going, fighting until the man was on the ground and the threat contained.

Only then had Evan dropped to the floor.

Tatum's first instinct had been to run to him.

But she couldn't. Couldn't deal with cleaning up that kind of mess again. Closing her eyes, all she could see now was the deep crimson drops of his life spreading across the floor.

"Ma'am, are you okay?"

Tatum looked up to find a paramedic standing next to her, his gaze scanning her for visible signs of trauma.

"Not me," she said, climbing to her knees and pushing the man toward the front door.

"Inside. My husband's been shot. Please, help him."

The guy gave her one more lingering look before darting inside the building.

She wanted to go back in there. And she didn't. She was so afraid. What if he was already dead?

God, she couldn't bury him again. Not again.

Another sob she couldn't keep down strangled her throat. Tatum pressed her hands over her mouth to try and stem the tide, but it was no use. The sounds oozed around her fingers, animalistic and broken.

Someone wrapped a blanket around her shoulders and led her to the back door of an open ambulance, sitting her down on the edge.

There were other response vehicles, another ambulance, a fire engine and several police cars. Their lights flashed, revolving in a kaleidoscope of color that made her head hurt. Her brain told her there must be sirens, but she couldn't hear them.

Hands moved on her body. She knew they were there, felt as they checked her for injuries she'd already told them she didn't have. They asked her questions. She answered, although she couldn't remember any of them.

She couldn't pull her gaze away from the doors.

And couldn't stop the sigh of relief when they finally wheeled a stretcher out of the bank. Evan was strapped down, but at least he wasn't covered with a sheet.

In fact, other than the equipment surrounding him, he looked okay—for someone who'd been shot.

His eyes were open and frantically searching the crowd gathering outside the bank.

"Tatum," she heard him say. "Tatum," he said again, his voice rising above the chaos.

He shoved against the restraints keeping him in place, pushing up on his elbows to get a better view.

And giving Tatum an unobstructed look at his chest covered with blood-soaked padding.

Her stomach rolled. "I'm going to be sick," she managed to say before someone shoved something plastic in front of her face.

"Sir, you need to lie back down so we can get you to the hospital."

"Not before I see my wife. Tatum!" he hollered. She could hear the panic in his voice. The man who'd just stared down an armed robber without batting an eyelash was worried about her.

And she was over here losing her lunch.

Pushing the bowl away, Tatum stumbled to her feet. They were numb. She couldn't feel them, but at least they held her up long enough to cross the parking lot to where the men with the stretcher had stopped.

The moment he saw her, Evan ceased struggling and dropped back to the gurney. He held out a hand, which she took.

His grip was strong. Stronger than she'd expected.

Tears stung her eyes, but she refused to let them fall.

"I'm fine, Tatum."

She shook her head. How could he say that? He'd been shot. Was headed to the hospital where the doctors would probably have to operate to get the damn bullet out of his chest cavity.

"I'm fine, Tatum. I promise." Using their clasped hands, he reeled her closer until she was practically lying on the stretcher with him.

Cupping her chin in his hand, he forced her to look

him straight in the eye. "The bullet just grazed my side. It's nothing. I've had far worse."

"If that's supposed to make me feel better, Evan, it isn't working."

He laughed, the sound breaking into a groan at the end.

"Sure, it's just a flesh wound," she said, trying to fight out of his hold. But he wouldn't let her go.

How was it, even with a bullet wound, the man was stronger than she was? Talk about frustrating. And a touch demoralizing.

"Let me go, you idiot, so these nice men can get you to the hospital."

"Not until I know you're okay." His voice dropped low. "I know this has to be freaking you out right now."

She hated that he knew her well enough to realize that. She had no secrets from him, which left her feeling completely vulnerable.

There was nowhere to hide, not from him. Not from herself.

"I'm fine," she lied anyway.

"You're not," he countered.

He leaned his forehead against hers. Tatum's eyes closed. She breathed deep, pulling in the sharp, spicy scent of him into her lungs.

How could something so simple both hurt and soothe at the same time?

God, she was a mess.

"I promise, baby. I'm fine. As long as you're okay, I'll always be fine."

She swallowed back the heavy lump threatening to choke her. Somehow she found the force to push out words she didn't really mean.

"I'm fine, Evan. I was shaken, but now I'm okay. Go to the hospital. I'll be right behind you."

He pulled back. His eyes, more golden than green, searched her face. She had no idea what he was looking for, but apparently he was satisfied because he nodded.

The men, who'd been waiting patiently while they had their moment, sprang into action. Evan kept hold of her hand until he couldn't anymore, his fingers finally slipping out from between hers.

She felt their loss like a tear deep inside.

The paramedics loaded him into the ambulance, one jumping in beside him. Someone smacked a palm on the closed doors and then they were gone.

And whatever she'd been using to hold herself together failed completely.

For the second time that day, Tatum dropped to the ground.

HE WAS FRUSTRATED, with everything and everyone.

The doctors were taking their damn sweet time getting him patched up and released. The groove the bullet had cut through his side hurt like a son of a bitch, but he'd refused the pain meds. Several times. The last thing he wanted was to be fuzzy headed.

It was just pain, and Evan had learned how to handle his fair share over the years. They'd given him a local when they stitched up the wound, but it was already wearing off. And he was still sitting on his ass in a hospital gown that showed way more of his skin than he was comfortable with.

He had no idea where his clothes were, not that they'd be much good considering the emergency room staff had cut them off his body, even after he'd started yelling at them not to.

No one had listened to him.

The bullet had gone through his shirt not his favorite pair of perfectly broken-in jeans.

He'd also asked for Tatum, but so far none of the nurses had produced her. He was going to be pissed if they were keeping her out in the waiting room when she could have been keeping him company—and from losing his mind.

He'd seen the way she'd fallen apart at the bank. He'd seen that haunted, hunted look too many times not to recognize it.

She wasn't okay, and he wouldn't feel comfortable until he could settle what had spooked her.

One of the nurses returned, a frown pulling hard on her lips and his discharge paperwork in her hand. "You know we really want to keep an eye on you for a little longer."

"I'm fine." He was getting tired of saying those words.

"There's a prescription for an antibiotic in here." She glared at him, fists balled onto her hips. She'd obviously missed her calling as a prison guard. "Get it filled and take it."

"Yes, ma'am," he answered, trying to suppress a smile.

She grunted, narrowing her eyes, but didn't say anything else.

They provided him with a pair of scratchy, uncomfortable scrubs to wear, but better those than marching out of the hospital with his ass on display.

He walked through the swinging double doors, half expecting to find Tatum waiting for him, so he was shocked as hell when Gage Harper pushed away from the wall.

"Where's my wife?"

"At home with her girls."

Dread sank into Evan's stomach, but years of training allowed him to school his features.

"She okay?"

"No, man, she really isn't."

Evan screwed his eyes tightly closed. Gage wasn't telling him anything he didn't know. But hearing the words somehow made them real and not just a fear manifesting in his head.

Clapping a huge hand across his shoulders, Gage said, "Come on. I'll drive you home."

The trip was silent, Evan's brain scrambling twenty different directions in an attempt to prepare for the worst-case scenario that he was likely walking into.

It was almost like prepping for battle.

When they pulled into the driveway and got out of the car, and Gage chose to stand beside his vehicle, hands balled into fists, instead of going up the walk, Evan's sense of panic deepened.

The front door opened before he reached it and Hope stood framed in the doorway. He thought she wasn't going to let him inside, but after several tense seconds, she stepped outside and out of the way.

"Everyone else left about fifteen minutes ago."

Evan started to walk past, but her hand on his arm stopped him.

"She's afraid, Evan. Scared out of her ever-lovin' mind."

"I know."

"No, I don't think you do. And I'm not sure she completely does, either."

What was he supposed to do with that? Hope wasn't telling him anything he didn't know. Tatum's fear had been a tangible thing, living between them, since he'd gotten back.

For a little while, he'd thought he'd broken past it. But in one quick moment the gulf was back. Right along with his worst nightmare—that eventually he wouldn't be able to find a way across again.

It was clearly not a good sign that she hadn't been at the hospital.

But Hope was waiting for some acknowledgement so he nodded his understanding. She squeezed his arm and offered a small smile that was far from reaching her eyes, and then let him go.

He walked into the still, silent house.

Tatum wasn't the kind of woman who liked unnecessary noise. She didn't play music or have the TV running for no reason. But usually there was…something. The sound of her chair squeaking as she rocked back and forth while she read a book. Or the clang of knives and pans as she puttered around in the kitchen.

Now there was nothing. Not a single sound.

"Tatum?" he called, walking through the den and into the kitchen.

She sat at the small table wedged into the corner, her gaze pulled toward absolutely nothing.

Crossing to her, he crouched beside her, resting a hand over her clasped fingers pressed to the table. Damn, she was ice cold.

"Baby?"

Slowly, she turned to look at him. It was the only way she acknowledged his presence at all. And when she finally did, Evan gasped, as if he had been punched in the gut. He wanted to double over. No, he wanted to throw up.

Dammit all to bloody hell. She was devastated. And he'd put that expression on her beautiful face.

"Sweetheart," he whispered. "I'm okay."

Lifting his shirt, he showed her the line of tiny stitches running along his side just beneath his armpit. "See, a scratch. They patched me up and sent me home."

Her mouth thinned and a spark of something lit in the back of her eyes. Thank God.

Well, he thought that until she opened her mouth.

"Sure, this time, Evan. What about next time? What happens then? When the next crazy lunatic with a gun manages to shoot straight? Or there's a kid with a bottle rocket. Or a handsy guy at the bar."

She was on a roll, words pouring out of her mouth so quickly they were jumbling together.

"I've already buried you once, Evan. I was broken. Practically comatose."

Tears washed her eyes and spilled over, but she didn't seem to notice.

"When you were gone, I finally understood why my dad did what he did. Up to that point, there had always been a part of me that was angry with him. Hurt. Because he chose the easy way out instead of fighting. Fighting for time with *me*."

Her hand trembling, she laid it softly across her heart.

Tatum's words gutted him, but it was the expression in her eyes that left him bleeding and defenseless. The mixed terror and guilt and anger and love and hope.

"But I understood it after they told me you had died. It took so much effort to wake up every day that not waking up suddenly sounded good. Just for the pain to end."

"But you didn't, Tatum. You didn't take the easy way out."

"No, but it was tempting. Way more tempting than I ever thought it could be."

She dropped her head back and stared up at the ceiling. "The problem is I don't think I have the strength to go through that again. To let you back into my life only to lose you."

"You aren't going to lose me."

"You can't promise that. And even if you could…"

Her gaze met his again, but this time there was no turmoil. Never once would he have expected to prefer that, but as much as it hurt him to see her struggling, it was far better than the cold, dead, blankness staring back at him.

"We're different people now, Evan. I realized that in the bank. Watching you confront that guy. Take him down. You could have killed him with your bare hands."

Evan rocked back on his heels.

"You were so ruthless and…focused. Hardened. You didn't hesitate at all. Not for a single second. You were ready to kill, and we both know it."

Of course he'd been ready to do bodily harm. The man had a gun pointed at her!

But that wasn't what she meant.

She was talking about him. About the monster he'd been afraid was locked away deep inside. The one she'd finally realized was there.

"What are you saying?" he asked, trying to keep his voice low and measured.

She didn't blink. "I think it would be better if you left."

It was what he'd feared all along—she would see beneath the polished surface of the man she'd once loved to what he'd been forced to become to survive.

And not be able to love them both.

So he did exactly what she asked.

He walked away.

15

FOR SEVERAL DAYS, Tatum managed to put up a brave front, pretending everything was fine. She rose in the morning, drove to Petals and acted as though it didn't gut her knowing Evan wouldn't be working beside her.

How could she have gotten so used to him being a part of her life again in such a short time?

She'd blown off the girls several times, but knew when the bell over the door chimed at ten minutes until closing time, it would be Hope, Willow, Lexi, Jenna and Macey. Her reprieve had come to an end.

Especially when she realized Lexi carried a huge bakery box, no doubt full of decadent, fattening, sugar-laden goodies. And Macey was double fisting bottles of wine.

Flipping the Closed sign and locking the door, they didn't give her a choice, simply ushered her into the workroom.

The top of the box was flipped open to reveal an assortment of treats, luckily none of them aphrodisiac chocolates because that might have sent her immediately over the edge. Willow broke out glasses and poured.

Fudge-covered brownie in one hand, glass of wine in the other, Hope hopped onto the counter, settling in as though she planned to stay all night. "All right, sister, spill it."

"Spill what?"

Willow arched a single, elegant eyebrow in her direction, and the wall Tatum had been holding everything behind for days cracked.

The tears started, quickly turning into ugly sobs, the kind with black mascara smears that required a box of tissues.

Lexi rubbed her back. Jenna gently extricated one wet, soggy ball of tissues to replace it with a dry one as needed. Hope crouched in front of her, holding her hands. They just let her pour out all the pent-up emotions.

When the tears finally slowed, Hope asked, "Feel better?"

She really wished she could say yes, but while some of the pressure in her chest had eased, the worst of it remained.

Because Evan was still gone.

And she was the one who'd sent him away.

"Not really," she sniffled.

"Wanna tell us about it?"

Tatum craned her head to look at Willow. Calm, cool Willow. How often had she wanted to be like her? Even when there was a crazy stalker after her, Willow had kept her head.

But that just wasn't Tatum. She had a quick temper and a sarcastic tongue. Her mouth often ran away with her, words spilling out before her brain could body check them into submission.

And Hope, so dedicated and determined. Once she

made her mind up about something, she tackled the task head-on.

"How do you do it?" she asked her friend.

"Do what?" Hope asked.

"Deal with the fear."

Everyone knew Gage Harper had a wild streak a mile wide, combined with a penchant for finding trouble. Even retired from the Rangers, he still found plenty of danger—skydiving and riding his vintage Harley, even if he did wear a helmet now.

Hope shrugged. "You just do. Because no one knows what tomorrow's going to bring. I was so worried about Gage being hurt in combat, but in the end, it was something stupid that almost took him from me."

"Shit happens," Willow chimed in. "And it isn't just our men. I mean, who would have expected me to be kidnapped and Tasered?"

No one, which had been part of the problem. None of them had been prepared.

"I guess my point is," Willow continued, "sure, Evan might take a few more risks than your average Joe, but bad things happen all the time to good people."

They had a point. Logically, she realized that. But emotionally… "Yeah, but none of you had to bury the love of your life."

Lexi wrapped an arm around her shoulders and squeezed. "No, thank God, we didn't. But, honey, I hate to point out the obvious. It happens. All the time. The difference here is you get a second chance."

"God forbid something did happen to Gage," Hope said. "I know I'd give anything to have him back. You have a flesh-and-blood miracle, or as close as I think you'll ever get to one, Tatum. And I'd hate to see you alone and unhappy for the rest of your life because you were scared to be grateful for it."

Hope's quiet words slammed into Tatum's chest. The pain of them spread, but behind that first wave was a warmth that thawed out the cold that had invaded her skin the moment she'd walked into the bank and stared straight down the barrel of a gun.

She'd gone numb, not out of fear for herself, but fear for Evan. Even before he'd acted, she knew exactly what he'd do.

Be the hero.

Because that's the man he was. A husband she was proud of. A man who put others before himself. Every single time. A man with integrity and honor who fought for those who couldn't fight for themselves.

How could she turn her back on a man like that?

She was a coward, and for a brief second, hated herself for the weakness she'd let rule her.

God, she hoped it wasn't too late to fix this.

Racing across the room, she rummaged around in her purse until she found her cell phone. And dialed a number she'd had for three years but had never bothered to use—Locklyn Granger.

ONE GOOD THING—the only good thing, really—about being in Charleston was that Evan had been able to do a little recon on the low-level thug from the cartel who had shown unexpectedly in the area.

Turns out, he really had been coming to see his family. The guy was nineteen, and when the cartel was dismantled, he'd managed to get through unscathed and hightail it out of Colombia, straight to a cousin on his mother's side.

It was just dumb, bad luck that the cousin lived in

Charleston, something no one had bothered to discover beforehand because the boy wasn't in the roundup.

It was probably going to be a very long time before Evan felt completely free and clear, but at least he'd finally stopped looking over his shoulder, waiting for a bullet to be buried in his back.

Although that was a small consolation considering he no longer had a job, a home or a wife.

He'd resigned from Special Ops, and no one had fought him on the decision. He thought the powers that be were probably secretly happy because now they didn't have to worry about what to do with him.

Nope, that was his concern now.

He'd rented a small apartment, though he had no intention of staying long-term. Maybe he'd go back to Detroit.

He probably should have done that immediately, but he wasn't ready to leave South Carolina just yet.

He wouldn't admit it was because of a certain dark-haired, green-eyed beauty. And while he'd caught himself dialing her number several times, he'd stopped himself from following through. Barely.

He was honoring her wishes.

The peal of his doorbell rolled through the small apartment. It sounded sick, stuttering halfway through and kind of petering out before actually finishing. Maybe tomorrow he'd take a look at the damn thing. Not that anyone ever stopped by.

Lock was the only person who knew where he was.

"I'm fresh out of beer, asshole," he yelled at the closed door as he jogged toward it. "So unless you came to replace what you sucked down last night, you can turn around and go back home." He finished the statement just as he yanked on the knob.

"You know I'm more a wine than beer girl."

Evan tried to suck in a deep breath and choked. The sound gurgled through his chest.

How had she found him? Why did it matter?

He stared at Tatum for several seconds, blinking rapidly and hoping desperately this wasn't a hallucination. Reaching out, he registered in some dim corner of his brain that his fingers trembled. But that wasn't important when he connected with the soft, warm satin of her skin.

A small, sad smile tugged at the corners of her mouth.

"Do you mind if we talk?" she asked.

Talk? "I suppose that depends on what you want to talk about."

Because if she was there to ask him for a divorce, he wasn't ready to deal.

But surely that was something she could have handled through lawyers without driving several hours to his front door.

Stepping back, he let her in. "Who's watching Petals?"

He had no idea why those were the first words out of his mouth. They were useless. He didn't care what the answer was.

"Willow's watching the store for me."

"That's nice of her."

"Hmm." She stared at him, unblinking, out of those mesmerizing green eyes. God, he loved her eyes.

"Evan, I want to apologize for the way I acted after you got shot. I was scared. Watching your blood pool on the floor…it brought back some terrible memories for me."

There was a space between them, not just physi

cally but emotionally. And Evan hated it. He refused to let it sit there anymore. Even if she pushed him away, he needed to touch her. Comfort her. If only for a second.

He pulled her into his personal space and tucked her tight against his body.

He expected her to stiffen, to wiggle away, fuss and growl. Instead, she melted. Her fists curled into the front of his shirt and she clung to him, as if she was afraid he'd vanish in a puff of smoke if she let go.

A small curl of hope unfurled deep in his belly, like the first sprouting flower of spring fighting against the cold.

She buried her head in his chest, and for several moments they stood together, unmoving.

Eventually, her fingers unclenched. Leaning back, she smoothed the wrinkles she'd put in his shirt. He could have told her he didn't give a damn, but didn't. He was too fascinated with watching her.

"Losing you was the worst moment of my life, Evan." She blinked back tears. "Worse than walking in and finding my father. Worse than watching my mother waste away from a disease that should have been curable. You were my rock through every difficult moment in my life, but when I needed you most, you weren't there. I know that wasn't your fault, but there was a part of me that obviously blamed you for it anyway."

"I understand," he whispered, the words hard to push through his constricting throat.

"No, that's not fair of me. I knew what you did as your job. I told you it was okay, that I'd be strong and handle the consequences, but I didn't. Not really. If I had, I would have welcomed you home with a cry and tackled you to the ground the minute you returned."

Scooping her into his arms, Evan walked the few steps to his sofa and sank onto the sagging cushions. Tatum burrowed deep, welcoming his arms around her.

This was the woman he remembered, the wife he'd longed to have back in his arms. His Tatum. Not the face she showed the world, strong and smart and a little prickly.

His Tatum was soft and vulnerable. And that vulnerability meant more to him because he knew it was something she gave to very few people.

"I love you, Evan. I never stopped. I've loved you since I was seventeen, and I want you to come home. We'll figure out a way to make it work. I'll figure out how to make it work. I just want you in my life."

Raining kisses over her face, he finally found her mouth and dove inside. The warm, hot recesses welcomed him in the way only his wife could.

"There's nothing to make work, Tatum. I resigned. They're letting me out of my contract."

Pulling away, she stared at him. "Really?"

"Really."

Before he'd even finished the single word, she was already shaking her head, silky strands of hair flying around them both with her vehemence.

"No. I don't want you to give up something you love—a job you're good at, and is important—just because I freaked for a minute. I'm a big girl. I'll deal with it."

"That isn't why I resigned. I…can't do it anymore. It isn't just you. I thought I lost a piece of myself in Colombia. I could feel my humanity slipping away.

You were the only thing keeping me sane and tethered to reality. I don't have the nerve to go back into that again. Not anymore. I'm too damn old for that shit now. There are plenty of hungry young guys champing at the bit to take my place. They'll be fine without me."

"What are you going to do?"

He shrugged. "Before I left town, Sheriff Grant offered me a position in Sweetheart. Apparently, he wants to cut back his hours and is looking for someone who could take over in a few years."

He watched Tatum's face for a flicker of reaction. She didn't give him one.

"But I turned him down," he said slowly.

"Why?"

"Because I didn't think you'd want me in Sweetheart."

"What if I told you I do? That I need you there?"

Evan's heart sped up inside his chest, thumping a little erratically. Could it be this easy?

"Sweetheart is a quiet town," he said, "but the job still has its dangers."

Grasping his face between her palms, Tatum leaned close. "You'd make a fantastic sheriff, Evan. Sweetheart would be lucky to have you protecting its citizens. It's more than what you do. It's who you are." One hand drifted down, stopping over his galloping heart. "And I love the man you are. I admire my husband and the selfless way he puts the needs of others before his own."

A beautiful smile bloomed on her lush lips. Her arms snaked around his neck, drawing him back to her mouth and she punctuated her words with an exclamation point of a kiss.

Breaking free, Evan murmured, "I love you, Tatum.

You saved me, gave me something to live for. Brought me back to life."

"No, Evan, I'm pretty sure, that's what you did for me. I was alone without even knowing it."

"Luckily, neither of us will be alone ever again."

He kissed her, pouring every ounce of love and heat and need into their joining. His hands roamed, wanting the feel of her smooth skin tingling across his palms.

"There is one thing we have to talk about," she whispered against his lips.

"Mmm," he murmured. "What?"

She fished in the pocket of her jeans and pulled out a simple gold band and the solitaire diamond engagement ring that went with it. When they'd married, he'd barely been able to afford the band. It had always bothered him that he hadn't given her what other women had, a diamond.

She'd never complained, but on their five-year anniversary, he'd surprised her with one anyway.

Tonight, it was her turn to surprise him.

Holding the rings out to him, she asked, "Will you put them back where they belong?"

"Absolutely." Taking them from her, he couldn't stop the lump from expanding in his throat as he slipped both rings onto her finger. Holding her hand steady, Evan watched the light catch the gold and diamond. "Perfect," he whispered before scooping her into his arms.

He headed for the bedroom and placed her on the bed, making quick work of her clothes. Kneeling beside her, he stared at his gorgeous wife. Her skin glowed. A fire lit her brilliant emerald eyes. But it was the love shining back at him that nearly broke him.

They'd been through so much—together and separately.

Though his body had survived the nightmare in Colombia, Tatum had been the one to bring his heart and soul back to life. And he would spend the rest of his days showing her how much he appreciated every moment in her arms.

Starting right now.

* * * * *

COMING NEXT MONTH FROM

Blaze

Available December 16, 2014

#827 SEDUCING THE MARINE
Uniformly Hot!
by Kate Hoffmann
Marine Will McIntyre wants two things—to get back to his unit after an injury, and Dr. Olivia Eklund. Olivia is very tempted, but she knows the sooner Will heals, the sooner he'll leave her...

#828 WOUND UP
Pleasure Before Business
by Kelli Ireland
After one mind-blowing night with Grace Cooper, Justin Maxwell demands more from his former student. But Grace has big plans for her future, and every moment with Justin puts that future at risk...

#829 HOT AND BOTHERED
by Serena Bell
Cleaning up an infamous guitarist's reputation shouldn't be that hard for image consultant Haven Hoyt. But once she gets her hands on Mark Webster, neither can resist their attraction—or the temptation never to let go!

#830 AFTER MIDNIGHT
Holiday Heat
by Katherine Garbera
It's New Year's Eve and überserious skier Lindsey Collins resolves to have a sexy fling. But bad-boy snowboarder Carter Shaw is determined to show her he's more than a good time.

REQUEST YOUR FREE BOOKS!
2 FREE NOVELS PLUS 2 FREE GIFTS!

HARLEQUIN®

Blaze®

red-hot reads!

YES! Please send me 2 FREE Harlequin® Blaze™ novels and my 2 FREE gifts (gifts are worth about $10). After receiving them, if I don't wish to receive any more books, I can return the shipping statement marked "cancel." If I don't cancel, I will receive 4 brand-new novels every month and be billed just $4.74 per book in the U.S. or $4.96 per book in Canada. That's a savings of at least 14% off the cover price. It's quite a bargain. Shipping and handling is just 50¢ per book in the U.S. and 75¢ per book in Canada.* I understand that accepting the 2 free books and gifts places me under no obligation to buy anything. I can always return a shipment and cancel at any time. Even if I never buy another book, the two free books and gifts are mine to keep forever.

150/350 HDN F4WC

Name	(PLEASE PRINT)	

Address		Apt. #

City	State/Prov.	Zip/Postal Code

Signature (if under 18, a parent or guardian must sign)

Mail to the **Harlequin® Reader Service:**
IN U.S.A.: P.O. Box 1867, Buffalo, NY 14240-1867
IN CANADA: P.O. Box 609, Fort Erie, Ontario L2A 5X3

Want to try two free books from another line?
Call 1-800-873-8635 or visit www.ReaderService.com.

* Terms and prices subject to change without notice. Prices do not include applicable taxes. Sales tax applicable in N.Y. Canadian residents will be charged applicable taxes. Offer not valid in Quebec. This offer is limited to one order per household. Not valid for current subscribers to Harlequin Blaze books. All orders subject to credit approval. Credit or debit balances in a customer's account(s) may be offset by any other outstanding balance owed by or to the customer. Please allow 4 to 6 weeks for delivery. Offer available while quantities last.

Your Privacy—The Harlequin® Reader Service is committed to protecting your privacy. Our Privacy Policy is available online at www.ReaderService.com or upon request from the Harlequin Reader Service.

We make a portion of our mailing list available to reputable third parties that offer products we believe may interest you. If you prefer that we not exchange your name with third parties, or if you wish to clarify or modify your communication preferences, please visit us at www.ReaderService.com/consumerschoice or write to us at Harlequin Reader Service Preference Service, P.O. Box 9062, Buffalo, NY 14269. Include your complete name and address.

HB13R2

Olivia pressed her hand against Will's chest. She could feel his heart beating, strong and sure, beneath her palm. "We can't do this."

"I know," he said. "But when I touch you, it all makes sense. All of the dark places are filled with light."

She'd made a vow to help him, and now she had to make a choice. If growing closer, more intimate, was what he needed, was she really prepared to refuse him? Especially when she didn't want to? Olivia smoothed her fingers over his naked chest. "We should probably talk about this," she said.

"I don't want to talk," Will murmured. "I want you, Liv. I need you."

Will spun her around and grabbed her waist, then lifted her up to sit on the edge of the kitchen counter. He pressed her back, standing between her legs and deepening his kiss.

He was hungry, desperate, and Olivia surrendered to the overwhelming assault. Will pulled her close and then, as if he were uncertain, held her away. But their lips never broke contact. Frustrated by his indecision, she furrowed her fingers through his tousled hair and tightened her grip, refusing to let him go.

"Tell me what you want," he whispered, his lips pressed against the curve of her neck.

Olivia knew exactly what she wanted. She wanted to tear her clothes off, finish undressing Will, then drag him to the nearest bed. She wanted to spend the day discovering all the things she didn't know about him and all the things she'd forgotten. Most of all, she wanted to lose herself in sexual desire.

This wasn't love, she told herself. It was just pure, raw desire…

Look for SEDUCING THE MARINE
by Kate Hoffmann,
available January 2015 wherever
Harlequin® Blaze® books and ebooks are sold.

HBEXP79831

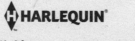